The Curiou
Black Swan Song

A Holmes and Garden Story

ANDREA FRAZER

The Curious Case of the Black Swan Song

ISBN 9781783756483

Copyright © 2012 by Andrea Frazer

This edition published by Accent Press 2014

The right of Andrea Frazer to be identified as the Author of the Work has been asserted by her in accordance with the Copyright, Designs and Patents Act, 1988

DRAMATIS PERSONAE

Staff at The Black Swan

Bellamy, Berkeley – owner of the establishment, ill-tempered with a roving eye

Bellamy, Philipa (Pippa) – general dogsbody and granddaughter of the owner

Burke, Tony – chef who is rigidly held to an inferior menu by the owner

Byrd, William – barman with a bit of a shady past who suffers for his name

Jacques, Tiffany – waitress and chambermaid, also local bicycle

Guests

Carrington, Niles – a businessman, flying under false colours

Garden, John H. – a man in search of his real self

Harrison, Jane – in dispute over ownership of part of The Black Swan

Holmes, Sherman – a man with an important decision to make

Hughes, Josephine – house-hunting in the area

Jones, Geoffrey – a man whose wife won't let him practise the bagpipes in his own home

Staywell, Casper – a previous guest who has an axe to grind

Members of the Local Ladies' Guild

Crumpet, Agatha – a respectable lady with a shameful past

Fitch, Millicent – a bit of a middle-aged tart

Guest, Marion (Mabs) – partner of Lebs Piper

Maitland, Margery – head 'honchette' of the guild

Merrilees, Anna – has a bit of a crush on the hotel's owner

Piper, Lesley (Lebs) – partner of Mabs Guest who knows Mabs has a crush on someone

Others
Budge, Justin – local estate agent
Pryke, Martin – Jane Harrison's solicitor
Streeter, Detective Inspector – of the local constabulary
Port, Detective Sergeant – of the local constabulary
Moriarty, Detective Constable – of the local constabulary

Prologue

The black and white frontage of The Black Swan hotel faced north across the High towards the rest of the pretty village of Hamsley Black Cross, its hanging baskets perked up by an unexpectedly sunny day amidst all the rain and gloom to which the area had fallen victim in this ghastly summer. The flowers, now not in danger of drowning, turned their faces to this glorious source of light and heat, and nodded their heads contentedly in the warmth.

The Black Swan, however, boasted more than frontage. Its shape formed a modified horseshoe which wrapped itself around a large cobbled yard at the rear, backed by the row of buildings that had at one time been stables, but by the present day had been converted to staff accommodation or, at a pinch, emergency guest accommodation – at a slightly lower nightly rate, of course.

It had started its life centuries before as a simple coaching inn, this one-time incarnation confirmed by the large archway that led from front to back, to allow egress to the horses and carriages that had once been its daily fare. It had over the years, cannibalised all of the buildings that were attached to it, whether Tudor, plain Georgian, Gothic revival Victorian, or Edwardian, until it had filled the whole block of buildings at this end of the village.

The main frontage had almost too many black beams to be believable, some of which had been much more convincing when they had sported their original ancient

1

oak colour. Tiny-paned mullion windows it had in abundance, as it did high Georgian sashes. It made a splendid sight on such a dazzling day.

Its tremendous oak front door stood open to banish the comparative gloom inside and welcome in the fresh warm air and sparkling sunlight, for today offered weather that simply could not be ignored in the middle of such a meteorologically disastrous summer.

Given that it had been built on what had been a major coaching route, its business had always been fairly brisk and, as new roads were built and other forms of transport devised, it maintained its popularity purely because of its pleasant architecture and beautiful setting. For Hamsley Black Cross is a very picturesque place and, being so close to the river Hams, brings the added custom of those who like messing about on the water.

The village worked hard to maintain its popularity, hosting a weekly Christmas market during November and December, a farmers' market on Wednesdays throughout the year, an artists' trail in the doldrums of January, and a flower festival in May. Anything else that would attract customers for local businesses was investigated and, in many cases, instigated by the ever-busy local ladies' guild, who worked tirelessly for their community.

Thus, Hamsley Black Cross thrived as it had done since historical times, and so did its principal hotel, The Black Swan, a building that if it were possible sat smugly looking down on all it surveyed, knowing that it was superior.

Inside, it had much to charm a guest, from its beams that sprouted mysteriously out of walls but went nowhere, and its huge inglenook fireplaces in which one could sit with a drink and survey the rest of humanity gathered there that evening. There was a splendid selection of little runs of steps that led up and down, seemingly at random, to differing floor levels, matched only by the inconsistencies of ceiling heights.

Strange little dog-leg corridors, apparently leading nowhere, also led the unwary guest astray, and corridors unexpectedly grew incongruous alcoves, the original purpose of which it was hard to guess. On the whole it was a maze of a building.

The Black Swan's swallowing of the adjoining buildings into its greater whole was evidenced by the number of staircases, mysterious little cubby-holes, and dead ends that littered the establishment. By the time the latter part of the twentieth century had had its wicked way with the building, with the installation of en-suite shower rooms and such like, the place was a veritable labyrinth for the unwary, and no handy signs were available to point the sadly astray, whether tourists or locals, towards their desired destinations.

Berkley Bellamy, the owner, liked things the way they were, and the frequent confusions of his guests gave him a great deal of silent glee.

Altogether, it offered twenty-eight en-suite rooms on two floors, and a further eight in the old stable block. Although business was not exactly booming in this dank and dismal summer, the place was well attended by local residents who appreciated its age, its charm, and its moderate prices for drinks and for meals, the latter somewhat uninspiring but undisputedly good value for money.

Chapter One

Friday

Today, The Black Swan would welcome three new guests, the first of whom was checking in as our story starts. Sherman Holmes had put his old-fashioned leather travelling case on the ground behind him as he carried out the formalities necessary to become an official guest, attended to by the establishment's superficially genial mine-host, who smiled as he swiped yet another debit card through his terminal.

He may not have many guests just at the moment, but Berkeley Bellamy had high hopes for the rest of the year, today's weather helping to confirm his predictions of a record summer to come. Although he was perfectly correct, the record wouldn't be for sunshine but for rainfall, and he also had no intimation whatsoever of what the near future held for either him or his establishment; or perhaps, didn't hold.

Taking the key to room number thirteen from a glassed cabinet behind the reception desk, he asked the new guest if he was superstitious, receiving the gratifying answer that it didn't matter what number the room boasted, as long as it was warm and comfortable and, above all, quiet, as he had some deep thinking to do, and had booked this short break to allow him to do that in the relative peace and quiet that he believed the hotel provided.

Handing over the key with another welcoming and reassuring smile, Bellamy gave directions to the room as slowly as he thought necessary, given their complication. As previously mentioned, no signs were available to help guests, and he had no plans to change the status quo. 'Go up this flight of stairs here, then turn left. When you get to the other end of the corridor, turn right, go up the four steps, left again, and your room is on the right,' he intoned.

Holmes was already flustered, living in an apartment as he did, with no complications or incongruities in its layout. 'Go up those stairs and turn … right …'

'No,' Bellamy corrected him. 'Turn left.'

'Right.'

'No, left.'

'I meant right as in "OK". Then down to the end of the corridor, you said, and go down some steps …'

As a young girl went to make her way across the reception area, Bellamy hailed her. If he waited for this silly old goat to get the instructions right, he'd be there all day. 'Pippa! Come here and help this gentleman to room thirteen, would you? He has difficulty with directions.'

'No, I don't,' Holmes interjected, for he felt quite affronted that a stranger should make such a sweeping judgement of him.

'Yes, you do! There you go, Pippa. Treat him gently.'

The young lady addressed as Pippa hefted Holmes' travelling case from the ground and called for him to follow her, as she bounded up the stairs with all the enthusiasm of youth. Abandoning his probably fruitless disagreement with Bellamy, Holmes did his best to follow this sprightly figure without losing her in the gloom of the interior of such an old building.

When Pippa returned to Reception, Bellamy curtly requested that she take over from him as he was 'gasping' for a fag, and needed caffeine to get him through to the evening. With a petulant little shrug, she slipped behind the desk and cast a glance towards the entrance, where another new guest was struggling through into the hall dragging a suitcase and wrestling with an unwieldy bag under one arm.

He introduced himself as Mr Jones and confirmed that he had booked in advance. Pippa took one look in the file marked 'Advance Bookings', which included any special requests, then booked him into room twelve; an activity she carried out with a dangerously mischievous twinkle in her eye. That'd show her grandfather, for such was the man who owned and ran the hotel. He'd not take her for granted again for a while.

Mr Jones, known to his friends as Geoffrey, was not such a dolt with directions as Mr Holmes had been, and trotted off with his burdens in complete confidence of finding his way without guidance. He had requested an isolated room when he wrote to book, as he had a very special reason for being without close neighbours on this little jaunt.

Following in his footsteps came a man wrestling with an enormous fluorescent lime-green suitcase, and wearing the most extraordinarily brightly coloured clothes. Pippa made no move to assist him, so taken up was she with thoughts of the little scenario she had just set up with room numbers.

'Mr Garden,' he puffed, as he finally reached the counter. 'I booked a bargain break on the telephone about a fortnight ago.' The words 'bargain break' nearly stuck in his throat, but he couldn't afford to pay normal room rates for this place.

'You're in twenty-seven,' Pippa informed him, handing over the key and eyeing his suitcase again. 'It's on the second floor,' she concluded curtly, then deserted her post in search of her grandfather, as she'd had enough of this 'covering on Reception' business for today.

Garden glared at her retreating figure and gave his heavy case a look of despair. Where else did he think they'd put him on a bargain break, but on the second floor? Just for a tiny instant he regretted the whole wardrobe's worth of clothes he had purchased especially for the next few days.

With a resigned face, he took a firm grip of the handles on his luggage and headed towards the nearest staircase, confident that he would have no trouble finding his room. After all, how difficult could it be to find a numbered room on the second floor? He had not stayed at The Black Swan before.

In his room, Sherman Holmes opened his travelling case and took out the carefully folded clothes to put away in the wardrobe and the chest of drawers. He was a tidy man who liked everything to be just so, and saw no reason to go about in wrinkled clothes just because he was away from home. As he hung two pairs of trousers in the wardrobe he was pleased to note that the room was also equipped with a trouser press. That was the ticket: keep a man feeling respectable while he was out of his normal environment.

Although he only lived a few miles away in Farlington Market, circumstances had forced him to come to a decision about his life, and he felt the only way he could really tackle the depth of thinking that was required was on totally neutral territory. Whatever decision he made, it was going to affect him to his dying day, so he had to give every aspect of it very careful consideration.

Holmes had recently been the beneficiary of a will belonging to a very distant relative that he didn't even know he possessed, and he was now faced with deciding what to do with his new-found fortune. Should he continue to live as he had done all his adult life until now, and just invest it, or should he try to follow his dream? At the moment he was in a quandary of disquiet about whether he really wanted any change to the even tenor of his existence. But then, that was why he was here in the first place, wasn't it?

As Mr Holmes came to the end of his unpacking, Mr Garden once more approached the reception desk, but from a completely different direction this time. He was rather red of face and out of breath because he had had, it seemed to him, taken a complete tour of the hotel, without, however, locating room twenty-seven. And now there was no one behind the desk to give him specific instructions.

As he stood there once more, Bellamy hove into view, refreshed by his fag and coffee break, and had to suppress a jolt of rage at the evidence that Pippa had deserted her post again without getting anyone to fill in for her. Breaking out into his most convivial smile, he gave Mr Garden precise instructions to locate his home for the next couple of nights, and said that where he had probably gone wrong was to take a left-hand turn on the first floor, then the steps up, instead of down, which would have confronted him with the wrong staircase to reach room twenty-seven.

Mr Garden didn't argue. He didn't have the puff for it. If he ever found the room and couldn't get himself back to this part of the hotel again, he'd just have to bellow for help until someone came to his aid. It was either that or a regular trail of breadcrumbs as he went about his daily business.

Mr Holmes was just settling down on the bed for a relaxing little read as Mr Jones in room twelve opened the mysterious bag that he had carried under his arm on arrival. With love in his eyes, he extracted his prize possession – his bagpipes.

His wife had had enough of him scaring the cat, making the dog howl, and the neighbours complain. She was tired of their children asking why Daddy couldn't do something normal like other fathers, and why he couldn't play something that the dog didn't know. In fact, she had forbidden him to play his pipes in the house ever again, and threatened, with complete sincerity, to leave him if he did.

He was now reduced to booking rooms for the occasional night here and there, and requesting that he may be placed well away from other guests, so that he didn't lose his touch or his technique. Practice, after all, makes perfect.

Mr Garden was just contemplating the last flight of stairs to his room, taking a little rest after his previous fruitless search and this repeat performance, dragging his over-sized suitcase after him, when Mr Jones inflated his bagpipes and began to warm up.

The shock of such an unlikely and strident a sound made him jump, and he knocked into his suitcase, which was parked at the very top of the previous narrow flight he had just climbed. As it rocked, swayed, and finally fell, he sat down on the top step of the next flight and dropped his head into his hands. It was probably easier to find the Lost City of Gold than to locate room twenty-seven in this place.

At the moment when the first caterwauling scream of the pipes had sounded out, Mr Holmes' body left his bed in a still vertical position, practically levitating, and his hands immediately went over his ears. What the devil was that insufferable row? It seemed to be coming from just the other side of the wall.

Grabbing his room key from the bedside cabinet, he rushed out into the corridor and began to bang furiously on the door of number twelve. A quiet room in which to contemplate a life-changing future, number thirteen was not, and he was incandescent with rage to find his immediate neighbour apparently strangling a cat.

It took Mr Garden another half an hour to locate his room, but he had taken a bit of a rest to eavesdrop on the furious argument that had broken out on the first floor landing; just as a way to pass the time while he got his breath back, of course.

Somewhat cheered by someone else's misfortune in this establishment, he surveyed his room with a rather jaundiced eye when he eventually located it, noticing that it was right up in the eaves and that, if he wasn't careful, he could go home with quite a collection of head injuries. There was, however, a magnificent pier glass over by the window, and his shallow character sent him straight to it to admire his new attire – his new persona, in fact.

His trousers were custard yellow, his shirt jade green, and his shoes were a sumptuous blood red. Gone were the office suit, shirt, and tie. Gone was the carefully slicked-down hair. This topmost of his adornments now stood in proud spikes and quiffs, marking him out as a trendy young man in search of the rest of his life, and his own true character. Whatever would Mother think if she could see him now? She'd probably burst into flames of self-combustion.

He would spend his time here working out a plan both to 'come out of the closet', and leave home, and a strategy for breaking these two devastating pieces of news to his mother, and it wasn't going to be a doddle. He'd pandered enough to her whims to keep him tied to her apron strings since his father had left her, and had indulged in all her hypochondriac manifestations, but enough was enough.

He was approaching his thirtieth birthday, and if he didn't do something positive to change the course of his life now, he would die in harness to her and his awful office job. Mother would just have to be told: there was nothing else for it.

He was resigned to the fact of resignation from his place of employment, for he was no longer willing to turn up for work looking like a middle-aged clerk. He wanted his attire to speak for who and what he was. He was also sure that he would, in the very near future, be looking for somewhere else to live, for, if his mother didn't explode with rage at the destruction of her image of her little boy,

11

she would go for hysterics, and still try to keep him by her side. He had a lot of decisions to make, and the only way for him to have the tranquillity to do that was to stay somewhere away from home, so that he could do his thinking uninterrupted.

Opening his enormous suitcase in the beautiful bright lime colour, he surveyed its contents with intense satisfaction. 'Out' were drab greys and unnoticeable navies from his life, and 'in' were stunning pinks, yellows, oranges, reds, and purples. No longer would he be a cypher, he would be a glorious butterfly who had just emerged from its protective cocoon. It would not be an easy transition, but he had girded such loins as he had to tackle his re-birth, and must now face up to the realities of what this involved.

As it was too early for lunch, he decided to go downstairs to the bar-cum-informal-restaurant where he could have a coffee and become more familiar with his surroundings. One never knew, but he just might meet somebody interesting engaged in exactly the same activity. Now it was time to try to retrace his steps to Reception, where he could get directions to his currently desired destination.

Good Lord, he couldn't be outside his own room again, could he? He'd gone down a flight of stairs. On the other hand, he'd gone up quite a lot of little collections of steps and, he supposed, with irritation, that they could have delivered him right back to the place he'd started from. Time for another go at this. Maybe he'd have to make notes if it proved too difficult.

His second attempt brought him out on the first floor, but with no visible stairs down from it, and he found himself outside a small library provided for guests, where he sat down in a tub chair to re-orientate himself. He must still be at the same end of the building, even though he seemed to have traversed its whole length. Maybe if he took the corridor outside the library he might come across some stairs that actually descended.

In this he succeeded, but they still did not lead to the ground floor, and he found himself outside the door of what was too small to be a guest room, given how close the doors on either side of it were, but from which voices could be heard in earnest conversation. In the hope that he may be able to secure help in his quest he approached the door, but his hand froze before he could turn the handle.

Inside, the voices were getting louder and louder, until he could discern exactly what was being said. One of the voices, the male one, stated, 'How on earth do you know? It could be anybody, knowing what you're like,' in a loud and menacing growl.

The voice that evidently was a woman's shrieked, 'How can you say that? You know how careful I usually am, except for that one time.'

Tiptoeing backwards about thirty feet, he began to approach the room again scuffing the soles of his shoes loudly on the floor, stopped outside the door from which there now was no sound, cleared his throat in a rather overenthusiastic way, and raised his hand to knock at the door. He had to get downstairs soon. The situation was getting ridiculous, and he feared that, once down on the ground floor, he would never return to his wonderful new bright wardrobe, just waiting for the next stages of his metamorphosis.

Before his knuckles connected with wood, however, the door opened and the man he presumed might be the owner, whom he had already met at the reception desk, came out, carefully closing the door behind him. This man, red of face and stout of body with not as much hair as he had once had, beamed a smile at him, and, before Garden could talk to him, shot off in the direction from which Garden had come. Fat lot of help he was, thought Garden, but remembered that there was still someone else in whatever space lay behind that door, and he was determined to complete his mission, or he could be roaming the corridors of The Black Swan for the rest of his life.

Taking his courage in both hands, he raised one of them to the wood and actually knocked on it softly this time. The door opened with a decided creak, a small female face leaning round it to peer at him, as if answering the door of what was now evidently a linen cupboard was something she did on a regular basis and nothing untoward at all.

'May I help you?' she asked in a quiet feminine voice, and risked a small smile of encouragement.

'I'm trying to make my way from room twenty-seven to the ground floor because I fancied a coffee, but by the time I find it, it'll be well past lunchtime. Do you think you could help me?'

'Of course, sir,' she replied, leaving the linen cupboard and closing the door behind her. 'If you'd like to follow me, I'll take you down there. I'm due on duty any minute to serve morning coffee, so we might as well go together.'

At the foot of the stairs, thankfully back where he had started his bewildering adventure of orienteering in this place, she headed off behind the scenes, and Garden found himself listening to a large angry man, in full flow of complaint at the reception desk with the man who had just exited the linen cupboard whence his guide and saviour had been incarcerated just a few minutes ago.

'I'm so terribly sorry, Mr Holmes. There must have been an unintentional mix-up with the room allocation. The man in the room next door to you should never have been given the keys to that room,' he blustered, 'He should have been allocated a room right at the other end of the hotel which is not fully occupied at the moment.

'Please accept my sincerest apologies for this oversight, which will be rectified instantly. In fact, I, myself, will see to it that his bags are moved, and I shall leave the key to his new room here behind the desk for when he is ready to take occupation of it. Please accept my sincerest apologies. The woman on Reception while I was on a break seems to have made an unfortunate error.'

Mr Holmes? Garden was fascinated by the name of the man making the complaint. Why, he would've given the moon and the stars to have had such a surname; but, no, his family couldn't even manage Watson. John H. Garden he was, always had been, and always would be, unless he had the guts to change his name by deed poll.

He'd been an avid reader of Sir Arthur Conan Doyle's Sherlock Holmes stories since he had been old enough to decipher them, and some of them he knew almost by heart. He must find an opportunity to speak to this chap to see if his name had been the instigator of a similar interest in him.

Maybe he could invite the man to join him for coffee, and just steer the conversation in that direction to see if he took the bait. Of his curious eavesdropping outside the first floor linen cupboard he gave not another thought, so distracted was he by his cunning plan to waylay a stranger and enquire into his reading habits.

The angry man with the oh-so-fascinating name made an abrupt turn of one hundred and eighty degrees and marched off in the direction from whence there flowed the delicious scent of coffee, and Garden, after giving him a lead of about thirty seconds, floated languidly after him, trying to appear cool and disinterested.

The Black Swan was a much-used meeting place for morning coffee and thus, most tables had at least one person sitting at them. Espying that Holmes, for the moment, sat at such a table, he approached rather diffidently and asked if he may sit down.

'Help yourself, dear sir. This place does seem to be popular with the locals, doesn't it; at least, I assume

15

they're locals. A lot of the guest rooms don't seem to be occupied at the moment.'

'Thank you,' replied Garden, glad not to have been rebuffed. 'I'm Garden, by the way; John H.'

A look of surprise crossed his new companion's face and he exclaimed, 'Good Lord! John H? Why, my name's Holmes: Sherman Holmes. Not a perfect match, but a bit of a coincidence, don't you think?'

Garden feigned delighted surprise. 'How extraordinary!' It looked like raising the subject of his obsession wasn't going to be as difficult as it had first appeared to him. 'I don't suppose you are familiar with the works of the great Sir Arthur?'

'Familiar? Why I could quote from a lot of his Sherlock Holmes stories. Are you, too, an aficionado?'

'Obsessively! I say, what a lucky meeting this is turning out to be.' Garden was ecstatic at finding such another as he, at least as far as taste in reading-matter was concerned.

'That means we can have a good old yarn about what sounds like both our favourite subject, with no one rolling their eyes and yawning,' suggested Holmes with a grin of pure joy.

'You get that, too, do you? We'd best make the most of it while we can, then. What's your favourite story? And do you like the other ones about the professor? And what about Sir Nigel?'

'It's Holmes all the way, for me, old son. I'm not into those other yarns – you know, like *The Poison Belt*; and Sir Nigel leaves me cold. *The Hound of the Baskervilles* – that's my favourite.'

'Mine too!' agreed Garden. 'The atmosphere is so well described that you could actually be there.'

'Couldn't agree more. The Grimpen Mire and the swirling mists really get to me, every time I read it …'

The conversation carried on in this vein through a

Danish pastry and two cups of coffee apiece. So engrossed was Garden that it was with only a languid interest that he noticed that their waitress was the young lady from the linen cupboard whom he had encountered earlier, in, to him, rather embarrassing circumstances.

As he was about to enter his thirties, he knew that the young were well-nigh impossible to embarrass, and just let the thought slip from his mind as he continued the (to him) fascinating conversation in which he had found himself happily involved, and when it had run its natural course, the two men turned to what the other was doing staying at The Black Swan.

'After you, John H., if you don't object to me addressing you as such,' offered Holmes.

Turning pink with delight at this mode of address, Garden took a few seconds to think, then passed this opportunity over to his new friend. 'You first, Holmes, as you are, after all, the senior partner.'

He felt a little frisson of fear that his reply may not be received in the manner in which it was intended, but he needn't have worried. Holmes had no real confidantes, and was as happy to set his problem before a perfect stranger as he would have been to write to an agony aunt under an assumed name.

'Righty ho! Here we go! I have come, unexpectedly, into a large sum of money. Don't go blabbing this all over the hotel, for God's sake. I don't want people sucking up to me and asking for a loan, or trying to bum dinner off me.' The man's voice had dropped to a low volume.

'Wouldn't dream of it, Holmes. Go on.'

'Well, I simply don't know what to do with it. I don't want to go mad and kick over the traces. Likewise, I'm bored to the back teeth with my job, and could do with escaping from the sheer grind of it. What to do, though? Should I just invest it and live off it? I'd die of boredom without some sort of shape to my day or week. What do you think, Garden?'

'Have you not got any secret ambitions that you haven't been able to achieve before? Something that you've always wanted to do and either never had the opportunity or the money?'

'Funny you should mention that. There is something that I've dreamt about since I was a lad, but it's too ridiculous even to contemplate,' Holmes confessed, looking a little shame-faced.

'Come on. You'll probably never bump into me again. What can it hurt to confess your heart's desire to me?' Garden was overcome by an insatiable curiosity to get to the bottom of what this new acquaintance really wanted out of life.

'It would sound too silly.'

'As long as it's not joining the Bluebell Girls and dancing the can-can in the Moulin Rouge, I can't see that it would sound silly at all. You can trust me never to divulge a word of what you say to another living person.'

Amused by this entreaty to confide in Garden, Holmes looked him square in the eye, and began to explain his life-long, if rather impossible, dream. 'Well, I'll tell you; and that's probably purely because of your name and our similar interest. I've always wanted to be a consulting detective like the great fictional character himself. I suppose today, the equivalent would be opening a private detective agency, but who on earth would need my services?'

'What a simply sumptuous idea! How on earth can you resist, if you've now got the wherewithal?'

'I'd feel such a fool when people found out what I was giving up a regular wage for.' Holmes was an extremely conventional and conservative man.

'So what! Not many people get to follow their dream, and if you have the opportunity and let it slip through your fingers, then more fool you.'

'You think so?' Garden had certainly given Holmes pause for thought.

'Absolutely! At least you have a way out of your humdrum existence. I'm trapped in mine and am determined to change my life, but it would probably destroy me financially and socially, and I'd have to go crawling back to Mother with my tail between my legs like a whipped puppy.'

'What on earth is it you want to do? Win the *X-Factor*?' asked Holmes, who wasn't totally alienated from the vicarious life of the twenty-first century: it was just that he preferred to spend as much time as he could in the Edwardian era.

'Are you mad? No, of course not.' Here, Garden's voice dropped to a whisper. 'I'm not gay and I'm not a transsexual, but I am a transvestite – that means I like to wear feminine attire. I just feel comfortable in women's clothes and I want to come out of the closet, but I live at home with mother, and she'd have a conniption and probably throw me out on the street, or tell me it's just a phase I'm going through. But it's not. I've known since I was a child that there was something different about me: I just couldn't get a handle on what it was until I approached puberty. Then when I did realise, I remembered all those cruel remarks my mother had made over the years about gay people and cross-dressers, and how disgusting they were – perverts to a man.'

'God! You are in a hole, aren't you?'

'If I come out, I might get thrown out. And the place I work in is full of intolerance of anyone who doesn't conform to what they deem to be normal. They couldn't use my 'hobby' as a reason to sack me, but they'd set something up so that they could get rid of me. So, you see my quandary? If I want to be who I really am, I have to give up home, job, and family. And I don't really have any friends, because I don't have anything in common with the people I come into contact with in my daily round.'

Holmes stood abruptly, announced that he needed time to think, and made as if to leave the table. Garden suddenly felt both dejected and rejected. Here, he had poured his heart out to a total stranger, and he had been rebuffed. Maybe the man thought he was making some sort of a pass at him, although he had explained that he was 'straight'. Whatever it was, he was quitting and going elsewhere to find company.

'Meet me here for dinner tonight,' said Holmes in a strangely strangled voice. 'Eight o'clock, if that would be convenient. I believe we have more to discuss, and the break will give me time to think things through.'

With a slight lifting of his spirits, Garden realised that his misgivings had been misplaced, and wondered what on earth the older man would have to say when they met again later that day.

Chapter Two

Still Friday

Holmes took himself off into the sunshine that was so rare a commodity at the moment, and took a stroll down the main street that led from The Black Swan through a street of shops which was separated by long, wide flower beds that bisected the road into two separate carriageways. At the point where the two carriageways became one, the last obstruction to their union was a church that sat facing the more secular way of life at the hotel.

The flowers in the long beds were in bloom, if a little battered by recent inclement weather, and made a bright slash of colour through the two rows of retail establishments. Holmes selected the carriageway to his right for the first section of his walk.

He had no inclination to buy anything, rather to turn his little window-shopping exercise into what would really be thinking time. Having finally expressed his situation to another human being, he needed time to ponder whether this experience had made any impression on the way he had previously viewed his circumstances, and realised that it did.

Because it had been vocalised, it now didn't seem such a madcap idea to throw up everything that until now had ruled his life, and throw his hat into the ring to see where fate led him. After all, he chided himself, you only live once, and if he passed up a chance like this, he might spend the rest of his life regretting it. Also, why put off until later what you could put into motion now?

If he took the chance now and it didn't work, he would have sufficient capital to pursue, perhaps, setting up another Sherlock Holmes society and mixing with like-minded people all the time. If he took the chance and it did work – well, he'd be in heaven, wouldn't he? Without even trying to rationalise the mechanics of realising his dream, he realised that he would probably now go ahead with it, just for the hell of it.

His conversation with that young man earlier had really galvanised his spirits. If Mr Garden – John H., as he had already begun to think of him – could face the tricky choices that life had bowled at him, then he, Holmes, had no reason for anguish and worry about what was a godsend, in the shape of his inheritance.

He was finally resolved. He would do it, and to hell with the consequences. And he might even be able to help out John H., who had been instrumental in him reaching this previously unlikely of solutions.

Arriving abruptly at the church, he stilled his pace and took a little trip up its steps and inside. He had no real idea what he felt about religion, but if anything other-worldly had been involved in guiding his steps to meeting the other man, it was certainly an occasion to give thanks, and he offered them now, to whoever or whatever may have been responsible, without his knowledge or comprehension.

John Garden sat on at the table which Holmes had just vacated and stared into space for quite a while, absent-mindedly ordering another pastry and coffee while he lost himself in thought. In his opinion, Holmes had no problem whatsoever. He should just go for what he thought was right for him. He, Garden, on the other hand, didn't have the backing of a whacking great inheritance to bolster up his situation, and although life was going to get very rocky for him for a while, after he had announced his intentions of being himself and not the man every other person in his life wanted and expected him to be, he'd probably live through it. Even his declaration for the love of colour in the guise of his new wardrobe would mark him out as different.

He'd had enough of being his mother's prize possession, and being at the beck and call of her whims over the years. He'd had enough of being a figure of fun in the office. No one ever said anything to his face, of course, but he had been aware for some time of sniggers behind his back, and disapproving faces made as he left a room or a meeting.

He'd booked this break when he'd had an almost overwhelming urge to wear a red silk dress into the office, and that simply would not do without a plan in place for how he would move forward.

All in all, he'd just had enough! He was going to do what he had intended to do as soon as this little visit was over, and the other people in his life could like it or lump it. If he ended up jobless and homeless, at least he would be being true to his inner self, and not pandering to other people's images of him.

He left the residents' lounge a resolute man, grabbed a newspaper from the reception desk, and walked outside to have a quiet read and a cigarette in peace. Let the world go screw itself. He was John H. Garden, and he would *not* conform to a way of life that was a lie. He would be his true self from now on, and see how that felt for the first time ever.

Sherman Holmes exited the church, absent-mindedly lighting his pipe, and began to make his way down the shop fronts on the other side of the flowers, glancing in shop windows as he walked, but taking little in. It was a good feeling to have at last made a decision about his future, but it wasn't long before he stopped dead in front of an empty plate-glass window and stared inside with a feeling of rising excitement.

The unit was empty and had a 'For Let' sign in its window. The estate agent's address was one that he knew was situated just across the road, because he had meandered past it at the beginning of his walk. What if? he thought, and smiled below his rather fine moustache. What if I just went and did it? He must find out whether the property was on a long or a short lease, whether it was just the shop frontage, or whether there was any accommodation provided with it. It was something he could achieve immediately, and he crossed the road, using a little pedestrian path that intersected the flower beds, to achieve this purpose.

Not that he wanted to move from his present apartment at 21B Quaker Street in Farlington Market, but it would be nice just to know the details. No, he was highly delighted with the address he had managed to obtain after selling the family house and finding a little hideaway for himself. It might not quite be 221B or Baker Street, but it had a nice ring to it, and was the closest he would ever achieve locally as an homage to his fictional hero.

The apartment itself was ground floor; one of three which had been converted from the large Victorian villa it had been built as. As the ground-floor tenant, he had garden access, a lovely drawing room, and two large bedrooms.

The name of the street was as a result of the Quaker meeting house that used to stand at one end of it, but had been so neglected as to fall into complete disrepair, with no clamour of local residents to fight for its rehabilitation. It had been demolished in the sixties, as had so many things that would never be seen again, but the road had kept its name, much to the pleasure of Sherman, who now made his home there.

Tapping out his pipe and returning it to his pocket, he

entered the estate agent's office with a determination either to achieve his dream or die in the attempt.

Meanwhile, Garden had read as much of his newspaper as he desired and decided that it might be a good idea to go back up to his room to freshen up before lunch. That meant, however, finding his way to said room again, and it was with a feeling of trepidation that he re-entered the hotel and stared around the entrance hall. Which way should he try this time?

With a decisive nod of his head, he turned right and walked down a corridor that looked promising, but the ancient place worked its black magic on him again, and he found himself in a cul-de-sac on the first floor which ended in what had presumably been the boot boy's room.

It was little more than a large cupboard, but lying inside, curled up on a discarded blanket, was a black miniature poodle, snoozing contentedly in the quiet.

Garden had an affection for domestic creatures and immediately approached the animal, intent on petting it and gaining its approval of his attention. With a wistful smile on his face, he stretched out a hand towards the poll of tightly curled fur, then screamed in pain as a mouthful of tiny teeth bit their way into the flesh of the ball of his thumb.

Retreating from the dog, he looked again, and it seemed still to be peacefully asleep. Now, Garden wasn't a man who learnt life's lessons easily, hence his problems with life in general and, trying again hopefully, the dog really did a number on him, managing to nip several of his fingers and produce some nasty scratches on his wrist that bled copiously onto the cuff of his new shirt – one of the jewel-bright ones that he had bought especially for this important weekend of decision.

Wincing with pain, and shock that such a tiny creature could inflict so much damage in so little time, he thrust his damaged hand into his mouth, and pulled at the cuff of his shirt-sleeve to try to avoid it getting too badly stained. While he was thus employed, a voice from behind him said, 'Naughty Sinatra! Don't be so horrid to the poor man,' and the young woman who had allotted him his room entered the restricted space, snatched up the creature, and pulled it to her breast to hug it.

'I'm so sorry,' she apologised, not looking in the least sorry, 'but what on earth are you doing in here?'

'I'm looking for my room,' he explained, wondering why this creature had mauled him so.

'Well, it's certainly not in here. And don't look so persecuted. He does that to everyone – except me. He's my little baby and he knows it,' she explained. 'Now, what's your room number?'

She conducted him to the door of his room on a route which contained only one flight of stairs and a couple of turns, and left him outside it, trying to manipulate his key without damaging his hand any further. This weekend wasn't going exactly as he'd planned it.

The only good thing that had happened so far was that he had definitely made up his mind about his future. Oh, and meeting that man Holmes, of course; although he probably wouldn't want to know him any more after what he had confessed this morning, even if he had made a date for dinner with him. He probably wouldn't show up.

Going into his bathroom, he washed and attended to his injuries, then placed his stained shirt in the bag he had brought with him to hold dirty laundry. It didn't seem to matter how positive you felt, he thought, life always had some other way of kicking you in the balls that you hadn't even considered.

He eventually had lunch served to him in his room, not being able to face the trek into *terra incognita* that he would have to make to gain either the formal dining room or the more relaxed one in which he had had coffee earlier on the ground floor. The rest of the afternoon he spent re-affirming his new course in life.

What were a few little nips from a tiny dog compared with what carrying on as he had been was concerned? He was more determined than ever to be true to himself, although he felt rather shivery whenever he contemplated a life of unemployment and homelessness. He could just be making himself a social leper.

Dammit! This was wishy-washy thinking, and it would not do. He'd go down for dinner this evening to meet that man Holmes, and if he was at all disparaging, he would just throw his drink in his face and walk away. No one was going to bully him or intimidate him ever again (although he didn't, of course, believe this deep down).

When he finally emerged from his room again, he was a glorious vision in a hot pink shirt and purple trousers, the very epitome of a fuchsia flower. His tie was lime green, as were his gloriously luxurious silk socks, and he felt a million dollars again. His hand was a sea of sticking plasters, but a well-known medicated cream had taken the sting out of his injuries, and he looked forward to the evening, in the hope that his companion of earlier was actually awaiting him downstairs.

Following a guest from the same corridor, he made his way down to the ground floor without a hitch, and turned towards the bar. It was only seven forty-five, and Holmes would be in the bar if he were to show up at all. And there he was, sitting at a table by himself, looking at what were, if he was not mistaken, estate agent's property details.

As he approached the table, Holmes raised a hand in greeting and waved at a chair for Garden to join him. He was smiling and evidently at his ease, so all Garden's worry about the other man's disapproval had been for nothing.

'Take a seat, Garden. I've made my decision, and I'd

like your opinion on what I intend to do. What will you take to drink?'

'Campari and soda, please,' replied Garden, sliding into a chair and letting his eyes stray again to the sheets of paper in front of his companion.

Holmes ordered the drink then turned to the information in front of him. 'I've had a little gander round the town this afternoon, and I've seen what looks like the ideal office for a small private detective's business: straight out of the hotel, go down the left-hand side of the flower beds, and it's about halfway between here and the church – the place with the "for rent" sign in the window.

'I've made an appointment to view for tomorrow afternoon, and I wondered if you would be so kind as to accompany me to give me your opinion on its suitability.'

'Ra-ther! So you've actually made your decision? You lucky dog.'

'Thanks. I think so too. Now all we've got to do is sort out your problem, and we can get on with the lives we'd prefer to live, instead of the one's we've let ourselves get stuck with.

'If you've really got a problem about where to live after 'fessing up to your mother, you can always come and stay at my apartment. I've got a spare bedroom, and you'd be welcome to bunk there for a while until you get yourself sorted out.'

'How generous of you. That, in fact, makes my decision a little easier. If I've got somewhere to go, I can get this thing over with knowing I won't be left to live in a cardboard box in the gutter, which my mother will probably think is the best place for me after what I'm going to tell her.'

'That's a little melodramatic, don't you think?' opined Holmes, as the waiter placed their drinks in front of them.

'You haven't met my mother.'

'She can't be that bad.'

'She isn't. She's even worse. Now, what time's your appointment tomorrow?'

'I'm due at the estate agent's about three o'clock.'

'I'll meet you in Reception – provided I can find it – at two-thirty, then, and you can show me where it is before we collect the keys.'

'Having a bit of bother finding your way around this warren?' asked Holmes, with a small smile.

'You can say that again. I feel just like Theseus in that Cretan labyrinth. I would leave a trail of crumbs, but I think the management may object. And I think I may have found the Minotaur in the shape of a vicious toy poodle that seems to reside in the old boot room.'

'Ah, that would explain all the sticking plasters on your hands,' Holmes said with satisfaction, another minor mystery having just been solved.

'Little sod had a right go at me when I was getting lost looking for my room. And you'll never guess what the little bugger was called? Sinatra! If only I had a pair of gauntlets with me, I'd throttle the little so-and-so. And I got blood all over my nice new clothes, too.'

'Never mind. The blood will wash out in cold water, and your hands will heal. There are much more important things afoot for both of us. Shall we go through to dinner, as we've finished our drinks, and you can take a look at these commercial property details?' Holmes spoke the last three words almost with glee.

'Actually, I'm starving. It must be all this emotional turmoil.'

When they had eaten, they sipped their coffee and discussed the suitability of the local premises, then Garden expressed his desire to go outside and have a smoke. The evening was warm, and smoking was absolutely forbidden inside the hotel.

'Splendid idea,' agreed Holmes, with enthusiasm. 'I'll

just nip up to my room to get my pipe. You toddle on out and park yourself on a bench, and I'll catch up with you in a couple of shakes of a lamb's tail.'

'It's not a meerschaum, is it?'

''Fraid not. Can't stand the sight or the feel of the stuff. No, I'm afraid I favour the model smoked by Basil Rathbone in his film portrayals of the great man.'

As they both rose from the table, the differences in their height became pronounced. While sitting down they had appeared of similar height, Holmes, a rather portly figure, proved to be of just less-than-average height, but long in the body. Garden, who was short in the body but stood at exactly five feet eleven inches, was decidedly long of leg, and towered over his companion from across the table.

They were, in fact, not just different in age-group, Holmes being a good twenty or more years the senior, but very different in their outward appearance. Whereas Garden had a long, thin face and very thick, wavy brown hair – now spiked with gel – Holmes had what might have been described as a 'chrome dome'.

He had hair only round the sides and back of his head. From his forehead to back beyond where his crown would have been there was hardly a follicle to be seen. He had inherited his male pattern baldness from his father who, since he was in his twenties, had divided his hair in a parting just above his left ear, and combed the strands from this side, which he had allowed to grow long, in a sad little brilliantined comb-over.

His son scorned this overt sign of being 'in denial' about his lack of hair, and always instructed his barber that he required 'a short back and sides: nothing off the top'. This was the cue for the barber to give a polite little titter, to acknowledge his customer's wit, although the routine was wearing thin after so many years.

Holmes made his way to the stairs to collect his oh-so-non-PC smoking gear and consequently it was Garden who heard the harsh voices emanating from the kitchen as he searched for the doors to the rear of the property.

'But it's bland, dated, and, frankly, unappetising,' shouted a voice he had not heard before.

'Who do you think you are, you jumped up little burger-griller? Who owns this place, you or me? I decide the menu and you cook it. Understand?'

'But we get so many plates returned hardly touched.'

'Nonsense! The locals love our food. Do you pay the bills for this place?'

'Of course I don't, but I could make it more profitable if only you'd let me be a bit more creative.'

'The locals like our fare, and I won't be swayed by a couple of dim guests who don't know good food when it's served to them.'

'They would, if only you'd let me cook it.'

'Terry, unless you drop this matter once and for all, you'll be getting your P45 sooner than you think.'

'Just you try it. I'll be off to a tribunal quicker than you could say "salmonella".'

'Don't push me too far.'

At that moment, the owner, Berkeley Bellamy, shouldered his way through the swing door and stormed off in the direction of the bar. Oo-er, thought Garden. He wasn't the only one with unresolved troubles.

Chapter Three

Still Friday

While back in his room, Holmes took advantage of the situation and 'used the powder room', then spent a good ten minutes searching for his tobacco pouch and pipe, which had mysteriously been hiding in his sponge bag.

On a bench in the garden, Garden was by now on his second cigarette and just enjoying the peaceful ambience of the place.

As Holmes exited his room, he caught movement out of the corner of his eye, and turned just in time to see a pair of shod feet shoot through an open window, to be followed by a cry of extreme anguish, a rather nasty squishing sound, then silence. He did not see anyone disappearing down the nearby flight of stairs, but he did become aware of a woman with a large, hairy mole on her face, leaning over his shoulder and breathing rather heavily into his ear.

'Did you do this, madam?' he asked, as much for something to say rather than in genuine interrogation, withdrawing his head from the open window to remove the dreadful sight below from his gaze.

'I certainly did not,' was the reply he received, with a little 'hmph!' of indignation. 'My name is Mrs Margery Maitland and I am the chairwoman of the Ladies' Guild. The committee is meeting in the guest library – often used for such purposes – and I just came out to see why our refreshments haven't arrived. They're over a quarter of an hour late, which is a very shoddy way to treat regular clientele.'

'I couldn't agree more, madam. Do excuse me, please,' spake Holmes, and made his way swiftly downstairs, after eying the bottom of the sash window, which was wide open.

Meanwhile, Garden had just been lighting his third cigarette, having got up to stretch his legs, when something big and heavy whizzed past his right ear, wailing, there was a very unpleasant sound, rather as if someone had dropped an over-ripe water melon from a great height, and suddenly his trousers had some very dark stains on them, and his shoes had some adornments of a pinky-grey stuff that definitely wasn't part of their design.

As Holmes had looked out of the window above, the young man gracefully folded in half and drifted down into a flower bed, dead to the world.

When Garden returned to his senses, he was lying on a Chesterfield sofa in the bar, Holmes sat in an upright chair beside him, a concerned frown on his face. 'I say, old man, it was lucky you didn't knock yourself unconscious. If you'd fallen the other way, you'd have landed in the rockery and could have given yourself a nasty crack on the head.'

'What happened?' asked Garden, then memory returned, and he made an unpleasant retching sound in his throat before asking, in a somewhat husky voice, for a glass of water.

'The owner of the hotel went out of the window near my room, and it sounds like he narrowly missed landing on your head. You could probably do with a stiff brandy and a nice cup of sweet tea as well,' advised Holmes, given furiously to think about remedies for shock.

'I'd rather just have the water, and perhaps someone to take my trousers to the dry cleaner's, and maybe sponge off my shoes.' Garden's face, which had been returning to something like its regular colour, blanched again as he remembered his shoes; his lovely new Italian shoes that he was wearing for the first time tonight. Looking fearfully down his body, he became aware that he was no longer wearing them.

'I took them off you and sent them to be cleaned up,' admitted Holmes. 'I hope that's alright.'

'Heroic in the extreme, although I don't think I can bring myself to wear them again. Is there any chance you could help me to my room so that I can get off these soiled trousers?' In retrospect, he recognised this as a good wheeze, to be led to his room and not to have to spend forty-five minutes looking for it, being savaged by what was probably a rabid poodle on the journey, all the time having to tolerate these disgustingly blood-stained trousers.

'The only thing I can think to do with them is burn them. I'll never be able to look at them again without thinking of what I saw ...'

Holmes, who did *not* have difficulty with directions, led his new acquaintance with unerring instinct straight to his room which, for a few moments, made Garden feel very inferior, then his attention was grabbed by a 'Do not disturb' sign on the door of the room next to his. Someone else must have booked in, so he might, in the future, have someone he could follow downstairs when he wanted the bar or the formal dining room.

Once inside, Holmes still with him to see him safely down again, Garden removed the offending trousers and held them out between finger and thumb, almost as if he were using a pair of tongs, and dropped them straight into the waste paper basket.

'Aren't you going to have them cleaned, then?' his companion asked.

'Absolutely not! I would be like Lady Macbeth, always

conscious that I – and only I – could still see the stains. I can't be doing with wearing a pair of trousers which would make me continually think, "Out, out damned spot". No, no, even though they're brand new, I simply can't face the things again. They'll be for ever haunted. I'll have to replace them.'

'Someone called the police while you were still in your swoon,' commented Holmes, more for something to say rather than for any other reason. Just what did one talk about when he was waiting for another man to put on a clean pair of trousers? If Garden ever got in the swing of his new life, he'd have to ask him.

'They'll need to speak to both of us, I fear, as the poor man landed right beside you, and I actually witnessed his feet going out through the window. There was also some woman there, although I can't remember her name, now. I'll have to mention that as well, of course.'

Garden was now, once more decently attired, and he turned to Holmes and declared, 'Here we are, just met, and we're already involved in a suspicious death. How's that for a coincidence?'

'Remarkable,' Holmes replied, his moustache twitching with excitement. 'I was going to ask you this tomorrow but, given what has happened, I think it would be better if I asked you now.'

'Asked me what?'

'How would you like to go into business with me as my partner in the private detective business? It could solve all your problems at one fell swoop. You could leave your job to work on this new one, and the flat above the shop could be made habitable – if it isn't so at the moment – for you to live in, and you could bunk in with me in the meantime.'

'Holmes, you're an absolute marvel. I say, will you come with me when I break things to Mother?'

'Of course I will, old man. A domineering mother is a

fearsome creature to face down.'

'You're a gem. I suppose we'd better be getting back down to the bar again. If this is going to be our first case, then we don't want to miss any of the action or the gossip.'

'I hadn't thought of that. Of course, we won't be paid for solving this death, but it would be a jolly good dry run for both of us, if you don't think that sounds too indecent in the light of the fact that a man lost his life here today.'

'Not at all. If we're going to be professionals, then we need to act in a professional manner, and that does not include squeamishness.' A fleeting memory of what had actually occurred earlier on passed through Garden's mind, and he blanched at the thought, thinking that he'd have to work on this aspect of what was to be his new career.

'If we go back via my room, I have a couple of small notepads with me that I thought I might need for jotting down the pathways of my decision process, but it looks like that is already done and dusted for both of us, so we can use them for making case notes in.'

'I say, how thrilling this all seems. I can't believe my luck,' chuckled Garden, rubbing his hands together and feeling back on form.

'Neither can I, young man,' agreed Holmes, similarly chafing his palms together. 'I get the feeling that we're going to get on like a house on fire.'

Back downstairs once more, the police were in evidence and they were taping off the scene outside, although interviewing had not started. The place was humming as news travels fast in a small town and nobody wanted to be left out of this *outré* occasion. The ladies of the guild had come downstairs to join the merry throng, and were having their refreshments served to them at the tables in the informal restaurant area of the bar. There were currently no seats available, so the two newly arrived men pushed their way through to the bar itself to order a drink.

As they elbowed their way through the crowd, there was a bright call of, 'Yoo-hoo!' and Holmes turned his head to identify the woman whom he had found looking over his shoulder when their host had, literally, dived out of the window outside his bedroom. She was beaming a smile of welcome and waving frantically for him to join them.

Garden also looked over at the woman beckoning to his companion, and offered to go to the bar while Holmes went over to see if he could secure them a seat with the ladies. 'What can I get you?' he asked.

'Make it a pint of bitter. This is a great chance for us to question that woman. I met her upstairs, you know, when our host went diving. She said she was with some women's group or other for a meeting, so we'll get the chance to pick all of their brains about the deceased.'

'Excellent idea, Holmes. I'll join you as soon as I can get served, although I'm fairly unnoticeable in a crowd.'

'Not in those clothes you won't be,' replied Holmes, before slapping a smile of welcome across his face and heading off towards the tables of ladies with determination in his stride. Holmes and Garden – Private Investigators, were just about to commence investigations on their first case.

When Garden got served, which he noticed he did with remarkable swiftness exactly according to his new partner's prediction, he made his way over to where Holmes was now seated amongst a herd of middle-aged and elderly women, rather like a short-sighted sultan who had either chosen unwisely when filling his harem, or hadn't traded in any of the older models for younger ones over the years.

There were half a dozen of these women, three of them crying into handkerchiefs. Another had a face of thunder as she sipped bitterly at her glass with tight lips, and two of them were whispering, heads together, about something that they didn't want to share with their companions.

'Ah, there you are, Garden. Allow me to introduce you to the members of the local ladies' guild, who were having a meeting in the hotel tonight. Ladies, this is John H. Garden, my new business associate with whom I shall soon be taking up offices in your fair town.'

One by one, they recovered their manners and held out hands of welcome to the newcomer.

'Margery Maitland, head of the Ladies' Guild. Delighted to meet you' – this was the lady who looked so discontented.

'Lesley Piper, but do call me Lebs. Everyone else does' – one of the ones that was in whispered conversation.

'Marion Guest. I'm known as Mabs' – the other secret talker.'

'Millicent Fitch. Pleased to make your acquaintance' – one of the ladies who had been crying.

'Agatha Crumpet, Mr Garden' – another weeper.

'Anna Merrilees. Delighted, I'm sure' – another one with a handful of handkerchief.

Garden put the drinks he was carrying down on the table while he shook all the hands offered to him, and some of the ladies grabbed a spare chair which had gone unnoticed and made room for him to join them.

'What sort of business are you in together?' asked Margery Maitland, almost challengingly, then looked round her as if to confirm that she could talk on topics other than the death of the hotel's owner this difficult evening.

'I'd rather not disclose that at this juncture, if you don't mind, my dear lady. Arrangements are at present at a very delicate stage.'

Nice one, thought Garden. They'd only seen fit to agree to a partnership a very short time ago, and Holmes hadn't even looked round the office premises out of which he proposed they should work. He only hoped he was right that there was a decent flat upstairs, or he'd be in a right pickle. Still, the man was long on imagination and short on the truth when he considered himself to be on a case, which was a good sign.

Garden was a bit of a babbler usually, and realised he would have to curb the enthusiasm with which he distributed details about himself to others – except about the things that really mattered. He'd talk happily for hours about music or books, especially those by his hero, Sir Arthur, and about any television programmes or films that he had enjoyed, but he'd better start to clam up now in case he let something slip. Here was another way in which he had to become a totally new person.

When he tuned back into conversation going on around the table, he became aware that Holmes had evidently gained their confidence, and was now engaged in drawing their life stories out of them. Clever man.

Margery Maitland seemed to be talking only about the guild of which she was head honchette. She made no mention of any family, the only other person being named in her tale that of the owner of The Black Swan, whom he gathered had rejoiced in the name of Berkeley Bellamy. What a mouthful.

Her view of him was through a very jaundiced eye, for she clearly had despised the man. 'He was so coarse and common, yet you'd be surprised what a position he holds – held – in Hamsley Black Cross. He is – *was* – on the parish council, a school governor, although what the man knew about education is anybody's guess – he wasn't one of life's brightest lights as far as intellectual capacity went ...'

God, she did – had – her knife into him, and Garden wondered what heinous sin he had committed to bring down such wrath and loathing on himself. She had been interrupted now, however, by three voices eager to speak in his defence.

Anna Merrilees cried out in outrage that such things were being said about the so recently deceased, and pointed out that Berkeley had been a man who looked after his guests well, whether residential or local, and always offered good value for money. He'd even allowed his premises to be used for charitable events in the past.

'But never, I noticed, offered to donate even a percentage of the bar takings,' interjected Margery, with a malicious smile on her face. Good heavens, the woman was practically dripping venom from her dentures.

Millicent Fitch joined in at this juncture to point out how sad it was that his daughter had died, and how gallantly he had stepped in, as she was divorced, in continuing the upbringing of his granddaughter.

Agatha Crumpet butted in to say that the man was sorely in need of an heir, as his daughter had been an only child, when Marion Guest – aka Mabs – stole the limelight with a paean of praise about what a lovely young woman Philipa Bellamy was growing into. She was only to be violently shushed by the woman next to her with whom she had been in cautious conversation – Lesley Piper – who now looked exceedingly out of sorts.

At this point, Holmes leaned towards him and said in low tones, 'I shall wander off at this juncture and see what I can get out of the staff. You stay here and ask them about when 'the incident' occurred. I think we can identify those who cared, those who didn't, and those who were indifferent from what we've heard already. See what you can do.'

He rose and made a small bow towards the ladies. 'I'm just off outside for a breath of fresh air, although you wouldn't think so when you consider that I am really going out to have a short puff on my pipe. I shall return soon.'

His attitude had gone down well, for there were

murmurs of opinions like, 'Oh, I do like a man who smokes a pipe.'

'Such a manly thing to do.'

'I just love the smell of the smoke.'

'My father always smoked a pipe.'

Garden girded himself up for throwing himself to the lionesses, in a conversational sense, and smiled all round, his stomach churning with a sudden influx of butterflies. He had started his new job.

Chapter Four

Still Friday

Very shortly after Holmes' departure, a loud and unexpectedly penetrating voice sang from the doorway, two words. 'Quiet, please.' Having been sung, they were instantly obeyed, and silence fell in the bar.

The person accompanying the unknown nightingale now spoke. 'Ladies and gentlemen, I am Inspector Streeter of the CID, and this little songbird is Sergeant Port. We are here to look into the death of the owner of this establishment, and I shall need to speak to you all. Should you need to leave the premises before this has happened, please leave your name, address, and a telephone number we can contact you on with my sergeant here.'

He was a bone-thin man with what looked like it could be a permanent drop at the end of his nose, which was beak-like, and red from the effects of a summer cold. Even on this warm evening he was dressed formally in shirt and tie, with a jacket held over one shoulder. His hair was steel-coloured, his face gaunt, and there was a steely glint in his grey flint-like eyes.

His companion was far easier on the eye, being of a rather more normal build, and also quite a few years younger. His face had a certain roundness to it which reminded Garden of a contented baby's, and he was more casually attired in chinos and a white T-shirt. He looked much more the pussycat of the two.

As this was going on there were mutterings afoot at the

43

table about getting another round in, and one of the ladies asked Garden if he would like another drink. Having been brought up with good manners, he immediately offered to buy the round. Suddenly, requests for orange juice or lemonade changed to calls for more alcoholic beverages, all with the word large in front of them. Here he was, hardly used to his new, bright, honest and investigative persona, and he'd already been rooked by the members of a ladies' guild, old biddies to a man – or woman in this case.

At the bar, where just a single member of staff toiled, he watched while he waited for another large order to be filled, noticing, as he did so, that a man in chef's whites had come in to speak to those customers who had chosen to eat in this more informal setting. Following a short chat with them, the man he presumed was responsible for the cooking in this establishment wandered over to the bar, went casually behind it, and pulled himself a half pint of best bitter.

'Oi, Burke!' hissed the barman. 'Get out of my side of the bar this minute. I don't go into your kitchen without permission and you shouldn't be this side of my bar, especially when you're in uniform.'

'Oh, piss off, Byrd! Written any good madrigals lately?'

The barman stiffened at this last remark, glared at his colleague, and asked, seemingly innocently, 'Introduced any original recipes lately, Tony?'

The chef nearly choked on his drink, and glared furiously at this evident taunt. 'Why don't you mind your own bloody business, William? I'm off back to my kitchen where at least I get treated with a modicum of respect.'

'So you think.' The barman wasn't giving in that easily – then he noticed Garden staring at him in surprise, smiled unexpectedly, and turned away from his tormentor. 'Sorry about that, sir. What can I get you?'

Having delivered his list and been served with his financially depleting order, Garden plucked up the courage to ask what had been going on with the man in chef's clothes.

'He picks on me because my name is William Byrd – a really long-ago composer – and occasionally I snap at him.

He's really restricted with his menu here, which I understand causes a lot of frustration and black moods in the kitchens, so I thought I'd have a poke back at him this time for a change. I'm sick of being the butt of his jokes about motets and madrigals, and other sorts of ancient music.'

'Good for you,' Garden congratulated him. This was the way to deal with people who took the mickey out of you, and he had just learnt something from this barman. That was how he needed to deal with disapproval and outright criticism of the consequences of his changed lifestyle. He was adamant. He would take no shit from anyone. Faeces would no longer be tolerated in his life.

He'd need to grow a spine first though, he remembered, realising what a coward he had been all his life. That, in fact, was why he found himself in this position in his late twenties. If he'd been brave and honest about who he was many years ago, he'd be accepted by now, or at least thick-skinned enough to deal with his detractors.

Pulling back his shoulders and straightening his back, he took up his heavily laden tray and wove his way back to the table where the old tabbies were sitting, with their tongues not quite hanging out.

The place had thinned out considerably when Holmes eventually re-entered the bar. Inspector Streeter and his colleague were steadily working their way round the patrons, but a lot had just passed on their details to Sergeant Port, and decided to call it a day, not wanting an interesting trawl for gossip to turn into a late night out.

Seeing that the others seated at the table were almost

ready for another drink, Garden rose, waved to Holmes, and made his apologies. 'I'm very much afraid I must leave you now, for I see Mr Holmes is back, and we have quite a lot to talk over in respect of our new business venture. Please excuse me.'

There were expressions of dismay as the women surveyed their nearly finished drinks, and one of them even tried to get him to stay just for another ten minutes or so – i.e. just long enough for him to get another round in – but he remade his apologies and sauntered off to where Holmes was standing at the bar.

'How did you get on?' he asked of his new business partner, sniffing greedily at the smell of smoke that still clung to his clothes.

'Meeting, later, in my room. What about you?'

'Plenty of gossip. I think I've managed to commit it to memory. I'll save that for later, too, but now, I've got to go outside; I'm absolutely gagging for a cigarette.'

'Stout fellow. I'll see if I can secure a free table for us while you're gone. I don't fancy going back to that gaggle of old women. Not good with women. Never been married, you know, although there's nothing dodgy about that – begging your pardon, of course. No offence meant.'

'None taken. As a sex, they're pretty daunting, aren't they?'

'I'll say. See you in a few minutes,' Garden said his farewells, and headed off towards a fix of nicotine, explaining his mission to a uniformed constable on the door, who was seeing that nobody tried to slip off without leaving contact details.

'I'll be right outside this window, where you can keep an eye on me,' he explained. 'You can come with me if you don't believe me, but I won't be responsible for my temper if you don't let me out.' The constable accompanied Garden to a bench outside the window and left him there, fumbling around in his pockets trying to locate his lighter.

When he returned to the bar, feeling a lot more relaxed and calm, he spotted Holmes at a table by himself in a far corner, and joined him, as he'd already spotted a glass on the opposite side of the table already waiting for him.

'Campari and soda OK?' Holmes greeted him, then leaned forward in confidential mood. 'I've had my talk with the policemen, you know. You'll never guess what the inspector's name is.'

'Streeter,' replied Garden, looking superior. 'I was here when he did a general introduction just after you left.'

'Well, don't you see what this means – what this purports?'

'No.' Garden didn't believe there was any point in giving a longer answer, as Holmes was dying to tell him something.

'Streeter – *Lestrade*. It's just like Holmes facing his old sparring partner in criminal investigation. Our business co-operation is meant to be – it's written in the stars. It's an omen, is that name.'

'If you say so.' Garden was unconvinced.

'Oh, come on. Can't you see how fate has conspired to bring us together, when both of us are at important crossroads in our lives? Both of us are avid Conan Doyle fans; we both need to move on, for varying reasons; we'd both like a crack at detective work; there's a perfect-looking place up for rent in the town. It's our destiny to work this first case and solve it before that lanky ape, Streeter.'

That 'lanky ape' proved to be right behind Holmes' shoulder, waiting for the opportunity to interrupt this urgent speech, and interview Mr Garden. 'If I may, sir,' he said in a deep rumbling voice. 'I understand Mr Garden was actually present when the body hit the ground. Do you gentlemen mind if I take a seat for a moment or two?'

At this mention of what he had witnessed when sitting outside earlier on, Garden lost all the colour from his face, and looked as if he were about to be sick. 'Feel free,' invited Holmes, suddenly gaining all the facial colour that Garden had lost in his embarrassment that the inspector had overheard what he had said about him.

'I'm afraid I can't be of much use to you,' Garden said, his voice husky with horror. 'I was just sitting on one of the many benches in the gardens, reading my newspaper and having a quiet smoke. I stood up to stretch my legs, when this thing whizzed past my head, there was an absolutely terrible sound as it hit the ground, and the next thing I knew, I was covered in yucky debris, and there was this body.'

'You didn't see whether Mr Ballard was pushed or whether he just fell?'

'I wasn't looking. As I just said, I was reading my newspaper, not looking about me.'

'And you didn't hear anything said – angry voices, or anything like that?'

'Nothing at all,' Garden replied.

'And you know I can confirm that,' interjected Holmes. 'I was up on the landing he fell from, and I didn't hear a thing until he went out of the window. The next thing I knew, there was this woman from the Ladies' Guild – over there – breathing down my neck.'

'And you really can't tell me anything more?'

'I heard a sort of wail or cry as he must have been falling, but it was all over in a couple of seconds, much too fast for me to be sure of anything except that he was absolutely stone dead.'

'Thank you for your frank co-operation, Mr Garden. Give your details to Sergeant Port, and I'll be off to speak to the ladies you say belong to the local guild.'

'He doesn't stand a chance beside us two,' commented Holmes, with a chuckle. 'We'll beat him to the murderer, hands down.'

'You're very confident, considering that we have no experience,' retorted Garden dubiously.

'No experience? Why, haven't we both read and re-read the Sherlock Holmes stories many, many times? What more experience do we need? Now, shall we finish our drinks and adjourn to my room?'

'Do you think we could make it my room?'

'Don't worry about finding it again. I'll see you back to it when we've had our little chat.' So, Holmes had sussed out his poor sense of direction. At least that boded well for his detecting instinct.

Chapter Five

Still Friday

When they got up to Holmes' room, the older man immediately got out his pipe. 'Steady on,' Garden warned him.

'Oh, this is a smoking room. Didn't you book one?'

'I didn't know they still existed,' replied Garden, immediately reaching into a pocket for his cigarettes and lighter.

'They do in these individual establishments out in the sticks that haven't been gobbled up by the chains yet,' replied Holmes, enthusiastically stuffing a dark tobacco mixture into the bowl of his pipe. 'Why don't you ask if yours is a smoking room and, if not, request that you be transferred to one?'

'I don't like to be a nuisance,' replied Garden.

'Then I'll do it for you. You must shake off this air of self-effacement – no good at all in a detective. You must have an enquiring nature and not be too shy to pry.'

Garden nodded his agreement as he held his lighter to the end of a cigarette. As he exhaled smoke, he said, 'This change of career will be very good for my self-confidence.'

'That's the spirit. Get everything you can out of a new experience. I feel like a new man since we came to our little agreement, and we shall view the prospective premises tomorrow afternoon. I can hardly wait. Now, what did you find out from the old dears?'

'From what I can gather, some of them might have been a bit sweet on the owner. If you remember, three of them were actually in tears when I joined them at their table. Another one of them had a look of such disapproval on her face that I thought she looked rather like a "hanging judge" – I wouldn't fancy crossing her. Oh, and two of them seem to be rather close, with one of them maybe being a bit sweet on the owner's granddaughter.'

'That was a good haul. Anything else?'

'The chef and the barman don't get on at all, and seem to be waging a bit of a war between them. What about you?'

'I managed to engineer bumping into a few people and, as luck would have it, managed to run into the chef as he was heading in your direction. He was happy to have a moan, and it seems that he is very constrained with the menu – Ballard won't let him experiment, or introduce anything on to the menu that hasn't been a firm favourite since the seventies, or resembles something from a school dinners menu.

'He, in his turn, has given up caring, and the food is now very mediocrely cooked and presented. It doesn't sound like a very happy kitchen to me.'

'It doesn't bode well for us eating here, either,' pointed out Garden.

'But we must, dear boy, so that we can eavesdrop. While we're staying here we must act like guests at Gosford Park, and listen in whenever we get the opportunity. We must become undercover spies.'

'Good grief.'

'You won't starve. Once we've made the pretence of eating in the hotel, I noticed there was a fish and chip shop close by which should serve us admirably, if the food has been too unsatisfactory. Although, I rather think that the menu will expand now, with the owner gone. I wonder who inherits?'

'Who else did you speak to?'

'A couple of the guests.' Here he consulted one of his small notepads. 'Ah, yes, a Mr Niles Carrington, and a Ms – *dreadful* title – Harrison. Very interesting conversations, both of them.'

'Dish the dirt,' ordered Garden, now thoroughly enjoying himself. This was the life – time spent with someone with a similar mind to his own (in most respects) and no one to kowtow to in a pecking order. He couldn't wait to get on with the other aspects of this new life, including moving out of Mother's house, although he quailed anew at actually explaining his new lifestyle to her. How easy was it to get hold of a suit of armour, and would this be considered a little over the top? But if St George faced up to his dragon, so should he face up to Mother.

He became aware that Holmes had begun to speak, and immediately wrested his conscious mind away from fire-breathing monsters and back to the case in hand.

'Mr Carrington says he is here on business, but this is not quite the case. This hotel, as is evident from the outside, consists of many smaller buildings which have been joined together over a great expanse of time. It would appear that this gentleman's maternal grandfather suffered financial loss when he sold a piece of the building to the Bellamy family about forty years ago.

'There was some sort of chicanery in the deal, and it was Mr Carrington's grandfather who lost out. His grandson has come here to scout out the property and try to find a way of making a legal case out of it now. He and his kin are evidently not fans of Mr Berkeley Bellamy, and the swindle, whatever it was, still rankles today.'

'And he just happens to be staying in The Black Swan when its current owner dies. I say, Holmes, you don't think it could have been suicide, do you?'

'Absolutely not! He simply wasn't that sort of man, in

my opinion, and I would expect someone like him to have left an accusatory note, pointing the finger to whomsoever or whatever had driven him to such a drastic action, if that were the case.'

'What about the other person – a woman, I think you said – that you "buttonholed"?'

Holmes again consulted his small notepad, flicking over a page as he did so. 'Jane Harrison; coincidentally, a very similar case. Her family has a long-running dispute over some of the land that now, ostensibly, belongs to The Black Swan, but she says it was simply stolen from them and added into the already large parcel of land that the hotel covers.'

'Another one who just happens to be a guest here when the owner pops his clogs. Well, well, well,' mused Garden, his interest definitely piqued. How many others were staying or visiting here with other grudges against someone who must have been a prominent man in the town?

'That disapproving woman from the Ladies' Guild – Margery Maitland is her name, if I remember correctly – was moaning about how many positions he held in local committees and things. She so obviously resented him: I could practically see the poison dripping from her fangs.'

'Now, now, young John H. No need to be fanciful,' Holmes chided him gently, slipping over to his wardrobe and extracting a nearly full bottle of malt whisky. 'Fancy a slug?'

'Please, Holmes. Where was I? Oh, yes, there were, I think, three of the ladies who were actually in tears – you must have noticed them before you went out for your pipe – so I suppose that there were a certain amount of crushes on such a – manly, I think is the word – man: a bit of hero-worship.'

'With maybe a bit of history thrown in,' added Holmes, coming out of the bathroom carrying the two still-tissue-wrapped tumblers that the establishment provided.

'Well thought out. We seem to be quite good at this, don't we?'

Both of them had availed themselves of the notebooks that Holmes had fortunately brought with him, so now each had a note of, not only their own, but each other's conversations during the evening, and now applied themselves to a good two fingers of fine malt.

As the inches evaporated into their willing throats, the talk turned to the circumstances of what had led them to their present situation. More malt followed, and the talk became a little rambling in places, a little too vehement in others, as is the effect of such an intake of whisky. The air above them had turned a hazy blue with the smoke they had both added to the atmosphere, and Holmes opened a window when both of them began to cough. It was only a small room, and could not cope with a pipe and someone who chain-smoked when he drank more than usual.

When they had each consumed about six fingers and Holmes was surveying the depleted level of amber liquid in the bottle with a rather blood-shot eye, they decided to call it a night. Plans had been set for the next day during this conversational jumble sale of personal information.

They would hang around the hotel in the morning in the hope of speaking to a few more people and do a bit of undercover eavesdropping. After lunch, they would slip off to view the office in the town then, to really get the ball rolling, they would call at John H.'s home and expose all to his mother. This would entail collecting his things and taking them to Holmes' apartment.

After that, they would need to get back to the hotel, as murders didn't investigate themselves, and that should just about fill the whole day. For now, though, the target was getting Garden back to his room safely, and getting a few hours' sleep to dissipate the effects of the large intake of alcohol, to which neither were accustomed.

'I'll see you back through the maze,' offered Holmes, with one eye shut to aid his focus.

'Thanks very much – very decent of you,' accepted Garden, similarly focussing with only one eye. If he opened both there were two Holmeses, and he didn't know which was the real one.

'Here, take my arm, and we'll walk together,' suggested Holmes, as a good wheeze for keeping both of them upright. Alone, they would probably stagger like drunken seamen.

They set off, turning left at Holmes' behest, wandering back and forth across the corridor, both of them frequently putting a finger to their lips and making loud shushing noises to keep the other from, probably, breaking into song. Finally Holmes drew to an unsteady halt, almost causing Garden to pitch forward on to his face, and pointed dramatically at the door in front of them.

''S room twen'y-seven. 'S your room,' declared Holmes with a flourish, waving an arm at the metal number on the door.

''S righ'. 'S my room. Con … congra … well done, ol' man,' replied Garden, a tear of gratitude forming at the corner of one eye. 'Couldn' have done i' withou' you.'

'Nonsense. Stout fellow. Could do anything. Goo' nigh'.'

'See you inna mornin'.'

Holmes turned and left Garden rifling through his pockets for the door key, happy that today had seen the formation of a momentous partnership. Garden just hoped he could find his key, and wouldn't have to crawl back downstairs in search of Reception for a replacement.

For Holmes, it was another story. The amount of whisky they had imbibed had robbed him of his sense of direction, and he tottered from corridor to corridor, staggering from side to side and all but pinging off one wall to bounce off the other.

Never before had he become this lost inside a building, and he managed to visit many fascinating places on this unplanned sojourn. He found the boot cupboard where Sinatra was still in residence, and remembered not to attempt to pet him. He found the small room in which the committee of the Ladies' Guild must have had their meeting. He found an unused gentlemen's lavatory with the Victorian fittings still intact, and gazed with wonderment at the decorated pans in the cubicles, one with a bee on the back for gentlemen to aim at.

He found a number of charming dead-ends, many of them adorned with framed pictures, as if to charm anyone who had the misfortune to find themselves lost in such a hopeless place. He also found Garden's room twice, not comprehending how he could have done that, when he had not tackled an ascending staircase. Without the courage to knock and admit his failed orienteering skills, he plodded on, losing hope by the minute.

Finally, he found the linen cupboard which Garden had described to him and from there, managed to locate his own room. He had never been so glad to see a bed with his belongings on it. What a day it had been – and tomorrow would be ever crazier, if his instinct was correct. A lot would be decided tomorrow, and things would be agreed that would affect the whole of his future.

Chapter Six

Saturday

Garden was the first awake the next morning, but not by choice. At the first wail of the bagpipes, Garden shot upright in bed and cautiously opened one bleary eye to look at his travel clock. Seven o'clock! And he didn't remember going to Edinburgh. Where the hell was he, and what the dickens was going on? And he suddenly realised where they had relocated Holmes' erstwhile neighbour, and assumed he was next door to him, Garden, because he was on a 'bargain break'.

For a minute or so he was paralysed with amnesia and panic, then he remembered, and rose immediately from the bed faster than would have been recommended, immediately reaching both hands to cradle his throbbing head.

The noise driving everything else out of his mind, giving him the strength to momentarily overcome the pain, he marched to the next door room and rapped very loudly on it. There was no response, and 'McCrimmon's Lament' skirled on. This time he both knocked and shouted. 'Hey, you in there, either you stop or I call the RSPCA.'

It didn't make any sense, but the volume must have disturbed the piper, for the appalling racket halted with an asthmatic and unmusical wheeze, and the door was opened by a man in full highland regalia, cradling a set of bagpipes in his arms like a beloved baby. 'Can I help you?' this vision of Scottishness enquired solicitously.

'Yes! You can shut the f*ck up!' roared John H., then blushed a deep crimson. He was not accustomed to using language like this and had surprised even himself with the vehemence with which he had spoken. 'I'm terribly, terribly sorry,' he apologised. 'That's last night's whisky talking. I was just wondering if you could desist for a while. I've got the most vile headache, and a very difficult and important day before me, so I need just a couple more hours' sleep.'

'No problem,' replied the tartan-clad man. 'I'm supposed to have been put in a room well away from other guests. I'll have a word at Reception when I go downstairs. For now, I'll just go through my fingering practise, and not blow down the chanter until well after nine o'clock.'

'Thank you. Make that ten, and I'll be eternally grateful.'

Garden slewed rather unsteadily back in the direction of his own room and staggered off, almost asleep on his feet, painfully aware that he was still drunk from the night before and hoping that a few more hours' shut-eye would render him sober enough for what he and Holmes had planned for the day – including the fearful spectacle of his mother looming out of his thoughts at him, breathing fire and brimstone for all she was worth.

Holmes cautiously opened an eye at eight thirty when the tea he had ordered arrived, the maid letting herself in with a pass key. 'Just put it on the dressing table,' he instructed her, shamefully aware that the room still had a cloud of fug just under the ceiling and that the glasses they had used, still reeking of what had been in them, sat on the bedside table also polluting the air.

The air also had that indefinable smell of man, partly consisting of iffy breath, stale sweat, and the ghost of unconscious farts passed while in the arms of Morpheus.

The first thing he usually did in his own apartment when he awoke was to fling open all the windows, even in the depths of winter, to air the space out for the following night. Unfortunately, he had shut the window the previous evening when they had got rather loud towards the end of their carousing.

The maid was either well trained or experienced, for she didn't flinch as she inhaled the foul miasma, placed the tray squarely on the dressing table, and wished him a good day before leaving him to wake up properly.

Rising reluctantly from under the covers, he tottered over to the pot and poured himself a cup of tea. His unexpected tour of some of the less-visited corners of the hotel was a bit of a blur, but he remembered well what their plan was for the day, and he needed to gather his scattered wits to deal with it head on.

He felt so dreadfully groggy that even his moustache drooped. It would take a full English breakfast and plenty of toast and marmalade to sort that out, probably accompanied by a pint or so of coffee, then he'd be back to full fitness.

As he was struggling to put on a pair of trousers that seemed to have far too many legs, there was an abrupt knock at his door, and he hopped to answer it to reveal the unexpected presence of Inspector Streeter, this time with an unrecognised young officer whom he introduced as DC Moriarty.

'Sorry about my state of comparative undress, only I'm having a bit of difficulty with my lower garments. Tamed the socks, only to have a fight on my hands with the trousers,' he stated, suddenly filled with excitement.

Moriarty! He couldn't make this stuff up! Lestrade and Moriarty together! He couldn't wait to tell John H. how the coincidences were heaping up, to confirm their decision to go into partnership as private detectives.

'We have had to ask for you to be allocated to another

room, Mr Holmes, as Mr Bellamy went out of the window just outside it. This part of the corridor needs to be taped off as part of the crime scene, and you won't be granted access again until we've finished. I apologise for any inconvenience this may cause you.

'Should you be kind enough to pack your stuff, a member of staff will collect it and move it to your new room, and you should enquire at Reception for your new number and key.'

'That's perfectly understandable, Inspector, as long as you point out that this is a smoking room, and I shall require another of similar ilk.'

'No problem. Now, about yesterday; you say you exited your room in time to see Mr Bellamy disappear out of the window? I just need to go through it one more time.'

'That's right, but a couple of seconds earlier would have been of more use, as it was only his feet I actually saw disappear – or his shoes, to be more accurate.'

'And was there anyone else around at the time that you saw, or could identify from hearing?'

'The only person I saw – and spoke to – was the Maitland woman from the Ladies' Guild. She suddenly appeared at my shoulder, though I've no idea where she'd come from. She said she was having a meeting with other members of the guild, so you should be able to find out from her which jack-in-the-box of a room she popped out of.'

'I shall need another word with Mr Garden next. Do you know, offhand, his room number to save me a trip back to reception? I do find the little runs of steps and the maze of corridors quite confusing, I freely admit.'

Holmes sent the men on their way to room twenty-seven, and began to pack away his possessions, after necking a glass of water with two Alka-Seltzers dissolved in it.

Garden was awoken again at nine o'clock, this time to a furious knocking on the door of his room. As he slept in nothing but a T-shirt, he fumbled around furiously for his underpants before answering the ever-increasing urgency of the summons.

When he had identified that it was the police, he asked them if they would mind waiting outside for a minute while he made himself decent, grabbed the first pair of trousers he could lay his hands on – which, incidentally were a deep episcopal purple – and pulled on a lavender and pink striped shirt before opening up once more and inviting them in.

Streeter didn't turn a hair at the man's bright attire, but the young man with him visibly winced as he surveyed such a colour scheme on a male body. 'May I introduce you to Detective Constable Moriarty,' began Streeter, then was puzzled by the wild giggling that greeted this simple statement. Garden, too, was not yet quite sober, and found the DC's name hilarious.

With a jolt of recognition, Streeter put the two names together and found out the course of Garden's mirth. 'Ha ha sir, very funny, but I can assure you that DC Moriarty is not a criminal genius, nor is he working for the baddies and against Mr Holmes.

'I have just had a word with Mr Holmes who saw Mr Bellamy embark on his ill-fated dive. I now want to go over again with you, as much as you can remember about his landing. You have confirmed that it wasn't a belly-flop.' Here, his constable groaned at the sick joke, drawing a look of disapproval from his superior.

'I told you yesterday that he must have landed on his head, although I didn't actually see him land. I heard him scream, but didn't have sufficient time to turn round to identify the source before I was covered in blood and … er, stuff.' Garden felt his gorge arise anew as he remembered what had adorned his trousers and shoes the day before. 'Please excuse me for a moment,' he mumbled, as he headed for the bathroom for a bit of the morning-after dry-heaving.

As he leaned his head down the lavatory pan, he heard the preliminary wheezing of a piper preparing to give it some welly. What a day, and he hadn't even got up properly yet.

When he re-entered the room he found both detectives with their fingers in their ears. 'What the hell is that cat-strangling noise?' asked Streeter in a distressed voice.

'It is the sound of Scottish music played enthusiastically on the bagpipes,' shouted Garden in reply. 'I'm going to have to ask that one of us is moved to a different room.'

'I'm actually glad now that they want independence. The only place in England that you can hear a sound like that is outside an abattoir,' commented Streeter in a loud voice.

'I love the skirl of the pipes,' roared Moriarty, 'but not usually at such close quarters. Fascinating instrument, are the pipes, and so many variations. I think my favourite are the Irish ones. And they have the benefit that you inflate the bag with your arm, so even asthmatics can play them.'

'Sod asthmatics. We'll catch up with you later, Mr Garden. I have sufficient respect for my sense of hearing to determine that this conversation should be carried out later in the day, at a place far removed from your room.'

There were others, too, in the small town of Hamsley Black Cross who awoke either in, or to, distress that morning.

Lesley Piper and Marion Guest were awoken by their radio alarm at eight o'clock, both momentarily amnesiac about what had occurred the day before. It didn't take long, however, before memory returned, and Lesley rolled over in their queen-sized bed to glare at Marion.

'I hope you're not going back to the hotel to smarm around young Pippa,' she said, stressing the word young, 'in the pretence of expressing your condolences. There's nothing worse than when an old dyke gets designs or a pash on a youngster. You're already making a fool of yourself, and it's got to stop, or there will be consequences.'

'I don't know what you're talking about,' replied Mabs, although she flushed with embarrassment.

'You think I haven't noticed the way you are around her, and you talk endlessly about how great she is, taking on the hotel with her grandfather. Well, let's see how she copes on her own now,' snarled Lebs.

'You have a sewer for a mind. And I'm sure Pippa will cope exceedingly well.'

'If she knew how you felt about her, she'd completely flunk it and leave the area as soon as possible.'

'I don't know what's got into you this morning. You're being perfectly horrible,' said Mabs almost in tears.

'Just making my position perfectly clear. I'm your partner, and this is my house. If you want to go on living here, count your blessings and don't go thinking the grass is greener.' At this, Lebs turned her back on Mabs and pretended to go back to sleep.

Garden decided to stick with what he had put on and, after a shave and a bit of a wash, he started on his way down to breakfast.

A wrong turning brought him to what he identified as Holmes' room, but instead of being able to go in and ask for company to find the bar-cum-restaurant, he found the whole end of the corridor taped off as a crime scene. This was a bit of a facer, and he about-turned to seek another route.

On his way he stumbled upon the girl from Reception, whom he now knew was the deceased owner's granddaughter, engaged in a rather heated discussion with Margery Maitland, both using raised voices in a bit to outdo each other.

'Ladies, ladies,' he interrupted. 'I'm sure it's only the tension created by the tragic events of yesterday' – he'd woken up a bit by now – 'that have caused you to fall out. I'm sure there must be an amicable solution to whatever you are in disagreement about.' Good Lord, he sounded almost like the father he barely remembered.

'I want to reschedule last night's committee meeting for tonight in the hotel, and Pippa here doesn't think she can accommodate me, although I don't know why, when there are simply dozens of little rooms scattered round this maze of buildings that would do admirably.'

'Not if you expect waitress service, there aren't,' snapped back Pippa Berkeley angrily. 'There simply aren't the spare members of staff. And I'd like to point out that, due to my grandfather's demise, I am now the proprietor of this establishment, so you can put that in your pipe and smoke it.'

Placing himself between the two battling females, now separated by himself as well as two generations, he enquired if a trolley could be loaded with refreshments, to be collected by one of the committee members.

'It could,' replied Pippa shortly.

'And would you be able to find someone willing to do that?' asked Garden of the older woman.

'Why, I'd be glad to do it myself,' replied Margery Maitland, with a sycophantic little smile at their unofficial referee.

'Well, that's settled then,' replied Garden, smiling too and taking advantage of this chance meeting by asking if one of them would be good enough to accompany him to the ground floor, as he was desirous of breakfast, and wasn't terribly good at finding his way around yet. He left the scene with both ladies for company, as neither wanted to give way to the other in accompanying this lone male to his destination. If they only knew the truth about him, he doubted they would have shown such keen enthusiasm. His female dress sense was better than theirs any day.

The slight rush of adrenalin from the police visit and the argument that had initially made him feel better had worn off by the time he took a seat at a table opposite Holmes, and he was only able to manage a nibble on a piece of dry toast and some black coffee. Holmes got on with putting away a plateful of fried things that Garden couldn't even bear to look at. Keeping his eyes firmly on the contents of his plate and coffee cup, he asked Holmes if he had had a visit from the inspector so far this morning, as his room now seemed to be out of bounds.

'Certainly did. They're having to move me, as the corridor outside my old room is part of the crime scene, so I've packed my bags and left them to be relocated. I say, did you have a visit, too?'

'I did.' Garden kept it short, as he felt another wave of nausea wash over him.

'Did you notice the name of one of his DCs? It's only Moriarty, which is absolutely stupendous don't you think?'

'Yes.'

'Are you feeling OK, John H? You seem a little green around the gills,' Holmes asked with concern, dipping a large slice of bacon into the yolk of his second egg and lifting the loaded spear to his mouth.

'I'm fine,' answered Garden curtly, trying to tune out the sound of enthusiastic chewing from the other side of the table. 'I think I'll just go outside for a little smoke while you finish up, then we can have a fresh coffee together.

'No skin off my nose. I've already had my first pipe of the day. See you in a minute, old boy,' replied Holmes, now savagely attacking a perfectly innocent sausage with his admirably sharp knife.

Garden stopped at Reception on the way out, noticing that Pippa was now on duty, and asked if his neighbour could be relocated. The man played the bagpipes, and was perfectly happy to do so in another location, and he knew his room allocation was restrained by him having booked a budget break.

'Oh, yes, that'll be Mr Jones. He's stayed with us before on a few occasions, and he leads quite a nomadic existence, from what I remember. I'll get him moved. He's used to it by now,' Pippa told him, with an impish little grin.

Garden then wandered out to the back of the hotel and lit up in the courtyard, but well away from the bench on which he had sat the previous day, which was taped off anyway – in fact, well away from the walls of the building. If he was under another window, goodness knows what could be thrown out of it and, sure as God made little green apples, it would land on him.

In the long past he would've been the fall guy over whom the potties would have been emptied of a morning. Life was like that, he found. The Law of Sod was alive and well and directing his life from the wings.

When he returned, Holmes was just putting down his knife and fork and reaching for his napkin with which to wipe his mouth. 'Feeling better?' he asked, from behind a mask of white damask, rather than the paper which he had expected.

'Much more human,' replied John H., and passed on the snippet of information that he had gleaned on his way downstairs.

'So, there will be another gathering of the guild tonight, then?'

'Definitely.'

'So we'd better have all our business concluded and be

back for that, if we can. I suggest we order another coffee and slip off to the guests' lounge, and see if we can't place ourselves, separately, in prime positions for a little bit of eavesdropping. We can pick up newspapers for cover from the reception desk.'

'Splendid idea,' replied Garden, who couldn't guarantee that he wouldn't indulge, quite against his will of course, in a little snooze while thus positioned. The residents' lounge, however, was nearly empty, as the police had taken possession of it, and so the two men decided to see if they could rearrange their appointment with the local estate agent for the morning rather than the afternoon, giving them a little more time to deal with Garden's mother and the moving of his worldly possessions.

Anna Merrilees did not wake until eight forty-five and, she too awoke feeling fairly normal. It only took a few seconds, however, before a great wave of misery rolled over her. Dear Berkeley was dead.

He was – had been – such an attractive and masculine man and she had had such a soft spot for him. If she'd ever fancied a husband, he would have been her first choice.

Millicent Fitch, also a member of the Ladies' Guild, awoke with tears on her cheeks. She had dreamed of the man she had, many years ago, had a one-night stand with. Although this had haunted her in her younger years, because behaviour of that sort was not so tolerated then, in her later years she had come to view it as the one romantic spot in her past.

Not that it had been really romantic; more frantic, but memory put a rose-coloured wash over everything, and now her memories were fond ones – most of the time. If only he could have quit his constant womanising with much younger females. She felt he had been making rather a fool of himself at his age, and had been considering having a word in his ear about behaving more like his age and not his shoe size.

Although she had shed real tears the evening before, Agatha Crumpet was more her usual self this morning, and the burning anger she often felt was again ablaze in her breast. When she considered what had happened in the past, Berkeley Bellamy had ruined her life, and she blamed him completely for what happened.

Young girls, at that time, knew little or nothing about stopping babies and, as the older and more experienced man, he should have been prepared to take precautions. He should have thought of the possible consequences of taking advantage of her, and not just laughed when she told him, several weeks later, that she was pregnant.

She knew how experienced he had been, for it had been he who had organised the abortion for her – and paid for it. Her father had been told that she was visiting an old friend, but her mother she had had to confide in, and things had never been the same between them for the rest of her mother's life.

Her own life was irreparably marred, and she had felt soiled for ever. Never had she got close to another man, feeling only fear, revulsion, and guilt at the very thought, and her tears had been an unexpected reaction to the man's death.

Casper Staywell lay in his hotel room that morning, exultant at the death of the man who had cuckolded him. He and his wife had stayed at The Black Swan for a few days a couple of years ago and, if he looked back honestly, his marriage had not been the same since.

Now that they were separating, he had finally learnt that she and Bellamy had had a brief fling during their stay, and that they had kept in touch ever since, occasionally meeting up for a bit of rumpy-pumpy. He was shocked and horrified at this information, and had vowed to come back and give the man a bloody nose.

Well, he'd certainly taken the ultimate punishment now and, although he couldn't tempt his wife to come back to him, at least he had the satisfaction of knowing that the man who had 'taken advantage of' his wife was dead. May his filthy soul rot in Hell.

Chapter Seven

Still Saturday

Justin Budge, when called on the telephone, said he would be delighted to show them round if they could make it to the office at eleven o'clock, as at half past he had an appointment with a Mrs Hughes from the same hotel, to view various properties. Mr Budge may have seemed free with his information, but this snippet from his agenda for the day was nothing compared to what he had to tackle later: something which was so well under his hat that, if he'd worn a wig, it would have been under that as well.

As it was now a quarter to the hour, the two newly minted detectives returned their newspapers to the reception desk and went outside to walk to the office, both of them lighting up, as they reached the exterior of the building. They were making hay while the sun shone, really, as clouds were slowly but unrelentingly rolling in, and it looked like a return to the previous wet weather so far this summer was on the cards.

'Wow! That looks just about perfect,' enthused Garden as he peered through the window, the estate agent not yet having arrived. 'I wonder what's at the back and upstairs.'

'I'm hopeful there may be further office space behind the front office, so we can have a public face and a private face where we can get on with our work in peace,' replied Holmes, relighting his pipe which had gone out, a frequent occurrence which he dealt with almost unthinkingly.

'And I could move into the flat,' squeaked Garden, who was only now realising that he could be about to inspect his future home, 'and stay with you in the meantime, which was a very generous offer, by the way. Thank you again.'

'Don't mention it, old boy. I'll be glad of the company, if truth be told. Aha! I think I see our chappie just crossing through the flowerbeds, *en route* to us now,' he concluded, pointing with the stem of his pipe at the figure of a young, fair-haired figure in a dark grey suit, and a smile that was visible even at this distance.

The figure checked momentarily and waved in their direction. 'Yes, that looks like him,' confirmed Garden, feeling a flock of butterflies start to flutter their wings in his stomach. This was the beginning of the rest of his life, and it was indescribably exciting as well as daunting.

Once more, a scaly dragon version of his mother reared up in his head and gave a puff of flame but, this time, he imagined himself mounted on a horse and in a suit of armour, sword at the ready. She was not going to win. For the very first time in her life, where he was concerned, she was going to lose the battle – and he'd finally become himself.

Justin Budge jogged over to them, arriving at their side not one whit out of breath, and looking one hundred per cent the fit youngster he was, curse him. He greeted them smoothly – a bit too smoothly – whipped the keys to the kingdom from his jacket pocket, unlocked the door, and invited them to enter their future together.

The inside proved to be everything that the outside had promised them, and there was already a built-in reception counter in place, with room for a small desk and chair behind it. There was also room for a few chairs for anyone who was waiting to be seen. The place was clean, light and airy, and had been well maintained.

Moving through to the back part of the building, there

was a good-sized room that stretched most of the way across the width of the front office, with plenty of wall space for filing cabinets.

'Wow!' was all Garden could find to say.

'Superb! Perfect!' Holmes was also lost for words at the ideal layout of the ground floor.

'It used to be an estate agent's office,' offered Budge with a smirk of superiority, as this business had evidently had to close due to the cataclysmic fall in house prices, and had, therefore, reduced the competition in the town now that business was tentatively on the up again. 'Would you care to see the upstairs as well? The access is from just beyond the back office. Did you notice the access door to the staircase?'

Neither of them had, so deep had they been pulled into their dream of the future that beckoned them so strongly now, and they followed him up to the first floor. Here was the ideal bachelor or starter flat. It had a small kitchen and shower room, a fair-sized living room and bedroom, and a box room that could be used for occasional guests.

'There is also access to loft space, although it hasn't a great deal of headroom, but would do for storage,' Budge explained further, but he didn't have to do a hard sell on these two. In fact he didn't need to do any sort of sell at all. They both thought it was perfect, and Garden was already working out where his furniture would go. 'Well, what do you think, or would you like me to leave you alone for a few moments so that you can discuss it in private?'

'Most considerate of you, Mr Budge. We'll meet you outside in a couple of minutes,' replied Holmes.

When he had left, the two men broke into enormous grins, and Garden started dancing round the living room, Holmes eventually joining in, although at a more stately level, and with a mite more decorum than Garden's disco fever. 'It's absolutely what I'd have designed myself,' declared the older man.

'Mentally, I've already moved in. It's absolutely perfection, and will solve all of my accommodation problems, not to mention how what we use downstairs for will solve my work problems,' chortled Garden, still prancing around.

'Let's just take a glance out of the windows to pass a bit of time, then we'll go downstairs and tell him we'll take it. I'll even offer to go over to his office and sign the papers immediately, then we'll go and see your mother.'

That soon stopped Garden in his dance of exultation. 'Stiff upper lip, old man. The sooner you tackle her, the sooner the situation is over with. And you don't even need to give her your new address which, for a while, will be my address.'

'I hadn't thought of that,' replied Garden, fascinated with the idea that he didn't even need to tell his mother where he was moving. He'd been so used to answering all her questions with the absolute truth – or nearly always – that he hadn't even considered withholding information from her to preserve his peaceful existence.

'You toddle on back to the hotel and I'll get the lease either signed or drawn up, if it's not prepared. I'll join you as soon as I can. I'll meet you in the bar,' said Holmes, with a twinkle of anticipation at what the future held in his eyes.

When Holmes left his office after a very satisfactory conclusion of their business together, Justin Budge rubbed his hands together in glee. It wasn't one of his habitual gestures, but with the thought of his next appointment, it looked like it was going to prove a very propitious and profitable day for him.

Although Josephine Hughes had put it about that she was looking over a house in the local area, she was actually a very wealthy woman indeed, and had her eye on

The Black Swan as a new business venture. Having Googled her, Budge had discovered that she was deceptively ruthless in her dealing in acquiring what she wanted, and he had no doubt that she would achieve her goal in this case.

The fact that old man Bellamy was dead only made the situation a great deal more interesting, and he was looking forward to putting up a smoke screen this lunchtime, while planning the preliminary approach to the new owner. In his opinion, The Black Swan was worth a small fortune and was in a suitably ripe position to be plucked by a slick and experienced woman of business.

Tiffany Jakes had turned up for work as usual, but she had been as sick as a dog before she left her humble abode. Her pregnancy was beginning to show, and she had had to wear a looser skirt and a roomier blouse so as not to give the game away.

Berkeley had been almost unbearably cruel when she told him about her delicate position, and had mocked her predicament, but he was dead now and she was carrying his child. She was going to give birth to the natural heir to the hotel, for he or she would inherit as a child of the recently deceased owner and not just a grandchild like the other heir.

Things had suddenly gone in a very good direction, although she had been devastated at first at the father's reaction to her plight. She had envisaged herself living in her little flatlet, an unmarried mother without the funds for child care and living off benefits, but now she would be the mother of the future owner of The Black Swan, and she would have to be taken care of, as would her child.

Two residents at The Black Swan were also almost dribbling with anticipation at the ownership of the hotel changing. Both Jane Harrison and Niles Carrington had 'found' each other the day before and exchanged stories about how their respective families were cheated over property transactions.

Now in alliance, they had determined to hunt down the chiselling git's granddaughter and find out who inherited upon his death. They would have justice for their families, one way or the other, and this was now the only course open to them.

His granddaughter, having been approached briefly by each of them in turn on the day of her grandfather's death, had gone into hiding this morning, and was planning to spend some considerable time closeted in the kitchen with Tony Burke, the chef, planning the new menu.

She knew he had been wanting to modernise and improve the food for some time and had met only with resistance from Berkeley. She knew of his enormous frustration, and thought that his ideas might improve custom and spread their reputation even further, and was determined to make this change to the menu one of the first marks she made upon the hotel's running.

She had wanted free rein to put her stamp – the stamp of youth – on the place for a long time, but her grandfather had told her she must wait until she had attended college first, and gained some sort of qualification in management, before he would trust her judgement.

She would not be going to college now. She would be able to take over and stamp her personality all over the business, and see how her ideas worked in reality.

Chef was in an excellent mood today, now that his plans for the hotel's food were to be realised, and he whistled as he went about his work while waiting for Pippa to keep her appointment with him. Life was good once more, and he intended to get full enjoyment out of it.

When Holmes got back to The Black Swan, he had no trouble locating Garden, who was sitting at a table near the windows looking out over The High. Holmes went straight to the bar and ordered two glasses of champagne – this was one of the very few establishments left that sold such a beverage by the glass – and went to sit down at the table with them, babbling about getting an official partnership agreement drawn up by his solicitor.

It didn't take him long to realise that things were far from well with John H., however. As he was saying, 'I just thought I'd get us a glass of champers to seal the occasion,' he became aware of the silly grin on Garden's face and the slightly glassy look in his eyes. 'You've already celebrated, haven't you?' he asked.

'More like Dutch courage,' the younger man replied. 'My mother is a formidable woman, and I'd die of fright if I had to have the conversation I'm planning to have with her stone cold sober.'

Holmes lifted a hand and began to click his fingers, eventually catching the eye of a member of the catering staff and ordering two dishes of the day to be delivered to their table. 'You need to put a lining on your stomach. If you eat something solid, it'll help to soak up the alcohol and sober you up a bit. Be a good chap.'

'Only if I can have the glass that you've bought for me as well.' Garden was digging in his toes.

'Only if you promise to have no more before we visit your mother, and agree to have a strong black coffee after we've eaten.'

'OK, but you're a hard man, Holmes,' Garden conceded, immediately scooping up the glass that had been brought to the table for him and necking it in one. 'Aah! That's better. Bring on the nosh.'

John H. had certainly made a beast of himself with his lunch and, when he had finished eating, Holmes had had to come round to his side of the table and wipe the gravy from his chin with a napkin. He had, however, given in and drunk two cups of coffee, and was a tiny bit less giggly than he had become when Holmes escorted him out to his car.

Practically pouring him into the passenger seat, he asked, 'What address?' which only brought out the playful in Garden. He tittered a bit and said, 'Shan't tell you. You've got to guess.'

'Lucky I took a look in the register, then, when I went to the little boys' room, wasn't it? I'm not so green as I'm cabbage-looking,' retorted Holmes with a smile of superiority. 'Sometimes I even live up to my name.'

By the time they pulled up outside an unnaturally neat, four-square bungalow in a road of similar dwellings, Garden was much more in control of his wits, and had broken into a cold sweat of fear. 'What am I going to say to her? I'm terrified,' he admitted.

'I've got that covered as well,' replied his partner, and produced a hip flask from an inner pocket. 'I keep this for emergencies, and I see this as qualifying as such. Here you are, just to recapture that Dutch courage you were seeking earlier.'

Garden made a grab for it like a drowning man at a straw, and took a long pull at the contents, before breaking into a fit of coughing at the sheer strength of the spirit. 'What the hell's in that? Meths?' he asked, trying to get his breath back.

'Polish vodka,' replied Holmes, trying to look innocent.

'And I thought you were a man who played by the rules,' said John H., looking towards the front door fearfully. 'Do I have to do it now?'

'The sooner the better. See? I'm getting out of the car with the keys. There's no reason for you to stay in there now, as you can't make it move. I'm just about to go up the path and ring the doorbell, so you'd better come with me or you mother won't have a clue who I am or what I'm doing on her doorstep.'

Garden was panicked into exiting the car and trotting up the garden path behind Holmes, his face a mask of sheer terror. Holmes pressed the bell and, after a couple of moments, the door opened slowly to reveal a woman who couldn't have been more than fifty. She was well made-up, her hair was as immaculate as the outside of the dwelling, and she was dressed with more than a flair for fashion.

'Mrs Garden?'

'Yes. How can I help you ... is that Johnny I see coming up behind you? Have you abandoned your special weekend early, Sweetie Pie?'

Holmes looked at Garden in confusion only to find him shaking with what appeared to be fear. 'Hello, Mummy,' he almost whispered.

'Aren't you going to bring your new friend in and introduce us properly?'

'Yes, Mummy,' John H. murmured, in a small voice.

'Do you mind if we have a quick chat together before we accept your kind invitation to come inside?' asked Holmes, totally confused. Was this really the dragon that Garden had been terrified of facing?

'Of course. I'll just close the door over, and you can ring again when you're ready.'

As the door swung to, Holmes rounded on his young friend and demanded to know what was going on. 'She seems a perfectly attractive, fashionably dressed, well-mannered woman. Where did you get this ridiculous dragon thing from?'

'She terrifies me! She seems so sweet, but I know behind her eyes lurks a cruel and merciless monster.' Garden looked as if he would pass out if he didn't sit down fairly soon.

'Do you mind if we go in and I form my own opinion of her? It could all be a fantasy that you have worked up for yourself. She may feel perfectly normal towards you.'

'Only if I can sit beside you and out of her reach. God

only knows what she'll do if she gets her hands on me.'

'I'm ringing the doorbell again, and stop being a ninny and follow me in when she comes back. If you're right about her, don't fear that I won't defend and rescue you, but I'm beginning to feel a bit of a chump. Have you ever felt like this before about anyone?'

'Absolutely not.'

Mrs Garden re-opened the door and waved them inside with a perfectly charming smile. She then overtook them and preceded them down the hallway and into a prettily furnished sitting room. 'Do take a seat and tell me what all this is about,' she requested. 'I don't really know much about Johnny's life, as he works during the day and I'm often out during the evening, making the most of the social whirl. We seem to have survived for years just leaving each other notes.'

Garden cringed into his armchair, trying to make himself invisible, while Holmes continued in his confused state of mind. 'I must admit to a tad of incomprehension, but the reason I have accompanied your son on this visit is because he has something he wants to tell you, and he felt that he needed some back-up.'

'Really? Do go on. I'm utterly in the dark.'

'John H. wants to tell you something really important about himself, and about some changes he wants to make in his life to make it more the life he wants than the life he is expected to live,' Holmes told her.

'John H? Oh, I think I see. Sherlock Holmes and John H. Watson.'

'Sherman Holmes, actually,' admitted the older man with a little blush.

'And I've never told Johnny how to live his life, but do go on.'

'I think John H. himself ought to take over the story here, for it is his to tell, not mine.'

Garden, looking hopelessly at sea in this embarrassing

ménage à trois, plucked up all his courage, screwed shut his eyes, and announced, 'I'm a transvestite, Mummy. I like wearing women's clothes.'

'Thank God for that!' exclaimed his mother unexpectedly. 'I wondered who'd been through my wardrobe and make-up while I was out. I'd noticed it on several occasions, but couldn't think of an explanation for it other than that I was losing my marbles. I never once thought of asking if it was you.'

'I'm leaving work and going into partnership with my new friend here, Holmes. We're going to take offices in Hamsley Black Cross and I'm going to work downstairs and live in the flat above. In the meantime, I'm going to move in with Holmes, and get out from under your feet.' Garden winced and screwed his body into a tight ball as if he expected her to physically attack him.

Instead, she clasped her hands together in delight and exclaimed, 'How marvellous for you. I know how you hate working in that office, and I've been convinced for years that it was time you found a place of your own and maybe someone to share your life with.'

'I'm not gay, you know,' Garden retorted. 'It's nothing like that.'

'I never thought you were. And why all the highly coloured clothing?'

'I just grew to love bright colours through trying on and wearing women's clothes,' Garden dismissed this last question as easily as swatting away a fly.

'So, what is this business you're going to run together?'

'A private detective agency,' Holmes answered, to give John H. a break.

'God, how exciting!'

'You knew I'd been through your things?' asked Garden, suddenly cottoning on to something his mother had said a while ago.

'I knew someone had been through them. I used to

fantasise that you had a girlfriend who was very interested in fashion, so you used to show her my clothes. Now I know it was you, quite a few things make sense. You never made many friends, ever. I suppose it was because you felt different.'

'That's right, Mummy.' Garden was five years old again.

'I know a couple of clubs where cross-dressers hang out. Would you like me to give you the addresses?' asked his mother unexpectedly.

Holmes accepted this kind offer, as the son of the house was just sitting with his mouth hanging open in disbelief. Mrs Garden suddenly piped up with, 'Shall I make us all a nice cup of tea?'

'That would be delightful, dear lady,' Holmes accepted on both their behalves. There was still a lot to learn here, and he needed to know more.

Garden was, by now, completely sober from the shock of his mother's easy-going reaction to what he had considered she would treat as dreadful news.

On their way back to the hotel, having arranged to pick up Garden's possessions when they had finished their stay there, Holmes felt moved to make a comment, although it was by no means meant as a criticism. 'This is the sort of thing that happens when people hardly see each other. Nobody can hear the tone of a note – or an e-mail, which you admit you've also used – and things are mistakenly assumed.

'In your case, you concluded that your mother disapproved of you to the nth degree, and avoided her company even more, becoming more and more withdrawn with your messages. You do see that, don't you?'

'Sort of.' Garden found it difficult to let go of the idea of his mother as a dragon.

'You need to go over in your head what life has been

like for the last few years, and then reassess how you may have over-reacted.'

''Spose so.'

'Your mother must have been very upset when your father left, but she said she'd done her best to build a busy social life since you had reached your late teens, and she expected you to do the same until you decided to fly the nest. I think you've seriously misjudged her.'

'Might have.'

'Look, we're going to need to stay on longer in the hotel – don't worry about the cost, because I'll pay. It'll be your first experience of being awarded expenses on a case. While we're still there, just think of the whole "mother" thing, while knowing that I'm always available to talk to if you need a sounding-board.'

'Thanks.' John H. seemed to be taking hard the elimination of his own personal demon, but he'd cope, given time.

'I know!' Holmes suddenly exclaimed. 'Let's take a run past my place so that you can see your room. A look at the old bachelor apartment might cheer you up.'

'Excellent idea!' Garden already had the bit between his teeth – anything to stop him thinking about Mummy.

Holmes pulled up in front of a row of older terraced properties, all of a good size for sub-division, and pointed at the black-painted iron railings outside his own building. 'There she is. And look at the red of that front door. Had to pay an arm and a leg to get the colour that smooth and shiny, but it's a real beacon, don't yer think?'

'I think it looks very business-like and welcoming, all at the same time,' agreed Garden, and they exited the car and mounted the few steps to the front door of the ground floor accommodation.

'The entrances to the other apartments are round the side, so it doesn't give the impression of a house in multiple occupation, which was a feature I rather liked when I bought it.'

'I can hardly wait to see inside,' almost panted Garden with enthusiasm as his new friend inserted a key in the lock.

As the door swung open, Garden was immediately transported to a bygone age. In the black and white checkerboard-tiled hall floor stood a venerable old oak coat-stand with antlers for decoration, and a large mirror for checking one's appearance before going out, or even answering the door. Below, an umbrella-and-stick stand stood for use by the respectable Edwardian gentleman. A couple of large prints on the wall were also contemporary with that age.

First, Holmes ushered him to a sitting-room that looked as if the great man himself had just popped out for an ounce of Bradley's best shag. Radiators for central heating were cunningly disguised, and there was an open fireplace with tiles contemporary with when the house had been built. Large battered chesterfields adorned the room, and even a violin had been 'carelessly' discarded on an old Georgian table.

A quick view of the kitchen showed that what looked very much of its age also managed to hide modern conveniences which it would be nigh on impossible to live without today. 'This is cunning stuff, you old fox,' commented Garden with admiration.

'Not too difficult, as I have sufficient funds, with only myself to take care of. And now, of course, nothing matters in the financial department. But I shall keep the old place on, of course. Not only is it convenient for our new business venture, but I've spent years getting the right address, and creating the interior. No, I'm quite happy here, and need nowhere else. Let me show you the facilities and your room. By the way, you're not allergic to cats, are you?'

'No. Why?' Garden was curious.

'Got myself a critter. It was a tiny, emaciated stray when I found it scavenging around the dustbins about three years ago, but we rather took to each other, and he's been my constant companion ever since. Had a cat-flap put into the kitchen window above the work surface, and he comes and goes as he pleases. Name's Colin. Dear old fellow.' Holmes had come over quite sentimental at this speech, and it showed Garden another side of him.

'I love cats, and shall look forward to meeting him. Where is he?'

'If I know my old lad, the lady's been in to feed him and he'll be stretched out on my bed. We'll go in there last, and I'll introduce you to him.'

Garden's room was light and airy, with a view of the back garden, the bathroom, again, in old-fashioned splendour of the latest manufacture. Finally it was time to meet the flat's other occupant, and Garden followed its owner into the last room available for his view.

Ahead of him, he heard Holmes' voice, no more than a coo, say, 'Hello my fine fellow, Colin. How are you today my little precious?' Garden rushed round the solid figure of his new landlord, already holding out a hand to stroke the dear little pussy cat, when a wild animal made a grab at his wrist with two enormous forepaws, and very sharp, needle-like teeth sunk themselves into the flesh of his hand, somehow avoiding the presence of the sticking plasters covering the previous attack by Sinatra.

He yelped with real pain, and Holmes immediately rushed to his aid. 'I say, I'm so sorry, old chap. He's not normally like that. You'll have to excuse him; he's had a very trying day today.'

Garden was about to agree, when he realised that Holmes was addressing the cat and not him at all. 'But what about my wrist and hand?' he whined, holding up the offending part of his body, which was beginning to drip with blood.

Turning his attention from soothing the cat, Holmes turned and asked in quite a cool voice, 'Please don't bleed on the bed covers. The bathroom is next door, if you wouldn't mind going in there and cleaning yourself up. You startled him. That's why he went for you. He's very nervous, you know, having had to fend for himself when he was tiny. You'll just have to get to know him and let him know you're not a threat.'

'I may not be, but he certainly is,' replied Garden, but he said it inaudibly, for he felt he had found Holmes' Achilles' heel. He was totally besotted by this huge grey and white tabby, and could see no wrong in him. With any luck, though, he would not have to stay here long, and would soon be settled in his own little flat over the shop, as it were.

Chapter Eight

Still Saturday

When they got back to The Black Swan, Garden suitably plastered up again, this being his second animal-related mishap within two days, there was a helluva kerfuffle going on, and the place was swarming with policemen and men in white suits wearing masks. Pippa Bellamy was manning Reception, and Holmes headed straight for her. 'What in the name of God is going on? I thought the police had just about finished what they needed to do.'

'There's been another death,' she answered him, without a flicker of emotion.

'Who this time?'

'That awful woman Margery Maitland. Apparently she went off to fetch the tray of refreshments for her precious committee meeting, and never returned.'

'How dreadful. Where was she found, and by whom?'

'In the boot cupboard where I found your friend the other day, with the trolley still beside her.'

'How had she been killed? I'm assuming it's murder, and not natural causes, judging from the number of officials on the premises.'

'She was garrotted with, they think, the electrical cord from one of the room's lamps.'

'Where has Inspector Streeter set up his interview centre?'

'In the residents' lounge, same as this morning. They'd only just finished getting through asking people about last night when they had to come back again. They only had a few hours away from here.'

'How ghastly for you.'

'Inconvenient, that's all, but it'll be good for business which, I would like to point out to you, is now my business, and I'm going to take it by the scruff of its neck and shake it until its teeth rattle. There are going to be some radical changes around here.'

That told Holmes, and he wandered away from the reception desk in the direction of the bar with a dazed Garden still in his wake. What a turn-up for the books this was, and how on earth did these two murders connect – if, indeed, they did? The web was considerably more tangled than it had seemed only twenty-four hours ago.

At least Streeter won't be on our backs over this one, though, he thought. We've been out all afternoon and the evening up to now, and the murder has taken place without our presence, fortunately putting us in the clear. I'm sure he was suspicious of us before, with one of us witnessing the dive, and the other the landing.

Garden wandered straight up to the bar and absent-mindedly ordered a double gin and tonic. Holmes, on *his* heels now after his few moments of speculation, asked William Byrd to make that two, and to bring them over to them. He then wandered off to a table by the door, took off his jacket, put it on the back of the chair, and, when Garden reached the table, told him he was going outside for a quiet pipe.

He desperately needed thinking time about what had happened earlier. Dismissing murders from his mind for a moment, he wondered whether Garden out of his mind, or had he just manufactured a phobia about his mother? Was his mother putting on an act? Was it a good idea to go into business with him? These were the questions that he pondered as he smoked outside the rear of the establishment in the courtyard.

After about ten minutes, he knocked out his pipe and went back inside, where he found Garden sitting with an empty glass and a calmer expression on his face. 'Drink up,' he said to Holmes, as he retook his seat. 'Do you know, I do believe you're right. I think most of the fear of my mother was actually manufactured in my own mind, by the guilt I suppressed about going through her wardrobe and chest of drawers and wearing her make-up.

'She does have a very busy social life with lots of friends, which she never had before Dad left. I think I've got this all wrong for years on end. Dad was the unsociable one, and all Mum wanted was to have a bit of fun. I do need to think this thing through a whole lot more, but I think a huge apology is in order, don't you?'

'I couldn't agree more. Sleep on it, there's a good chap. I'll just get us another, and we can talk about the latest murder, if that would distract you until you've got some privacy.'

'Good idea.'

When he got back to the table, he found that his companion had been joined by two of the women they had met the previous evening – the two slightly younger ones who didn't look as if they had just been exhumed.

'Good evening, ladies. I was so sorry to hear about your friend. It must have been awful when she just didn't come back with the refreshments.'

'Mabs Guest,' said one, holding out her hand to be shaken.

'Lebs Piper,' said the other, doing likewise. 'We meet again. It was a terrible shock for us all, especially after what happened only yesterday.'

'At first we thought she'd nipped off to a quiet corner to stuff all the best cakes and biscuits,' Mabs continued their story.

'Then we really began to worry when she'd been gone over half an hour.' Lebs took the verbal shot and returned it with complete accuracy and skill.

'So we got Pippa and asked her if she could take a look for her, in case she'd tripped with the trolley and, perhaps, sprained an ankle, or something silly like that.'

It was like watching Wimbledon, the two men's heads turning from one side to the other as the women took it in turns to elaborate on the story.

'Well, you would go rushing off to dear Pippa, wouldn't you? You do have a rather embarrassing soft spot for her. I say, get off to the bar and get us another one. It's your turn, I believe,' ordered Lebs in quite a harsh voice then, turning to her two gentlemen companions, she managed a small smile and said, 'Just for the shock, you understand.'

Holmes certainly understood. These two had been in the bar for a while and had imbibed quite a lot of medicine for their condition and, if he and Garden were really lucky, there may be a few home truths to come out. Of one thing he was certain, however – these two were a couple, and one of them was jealous of the other's 'pash' on Pippa Bellamy.

In Mabs' absence, Lebs did become rather confidential, and leaned towards them so that she could confide something, but *sotto voce*. 'That Margery Maitland was a snotty old bag, but I do know a secret that I haven't even passed on to Mabs.'

Here she paused and looked from side to side, so exactly like a spy in a third-rate movie that Holmes almost laughed. Garden was still lost in thought. 'My father was the local doctor – a very respected man in the town, and when Margery was very much younger and Father was still in his prime, she came to him because she had got herself into trouble.

'There, I thought you'd be shocked. It was just before the Act was passed, and she wanted him to help her out – probably far too scared to go the back-street route, and I don't blame her. The whole thing was ruthlessly suppressed, and she was said to be visiting a maiden aunt in London while she was having it done.

'Father never told me this until he was virtually on his death bed, and I suppose the idea of patient confidentiality had flown out of the window in his desire to be able to leave behind him a few juicy snippets. You'll never guess who the father was.'

'We're not from around here ... Lebs,' Holmes reminded her.

'It was Berkeley Bellamy. She'd lost her cherry to the local Casanova, got herself in the club, and she's hated him ever since. You must have noticed the hatchet-faced expression she wore when the guild committee was here. Well, that was only for him, and she never looked that grim anywhere else. What do you think of that, then?'

'I'm shocked, dear lady, but I hardly see that it has anything to do with the case in hand, as Ms Maitland has also fallen victim to whoever is responsible for these two murders.'

Mabs returned at that point with a tray holding four glasses. 'I thought I'd get us all another,' she announced, passing the tray round so that everyone could help themselves.

'How very kind of you, dear lady,' Holmes thanked them, noticing the while that Garden was still off in another world. 'Why don't you go on up, old man. I'm not ready yet, but you've had a very trying day, and I think you'd be better off in your room, even if you're not yet ready to go to sleep.'

'Yes, Holmes. Goodnight all.' Garden stood up like a zombie, drained his new glass and exited the bar, working so much on auto-pilot that he didn't even consider the difficulties of locating his room, and consequently found it without any difficulty at all. He simply must have been trying too hard in the past.

He'd only been in there a couple of minutes, sitting on the bed still in a bit of a daze at the turn of events since visiting his old home, when there was a peremptory knock on the door, and he opened it to reveal a police presence. 'Do you mind if we have a word with you?' asked Inspector Streeter, his voice and face completely devoid of expression.

Back in the bar, the ladies noticed that it was past their bedtime, and collected their handbags before bidding Holmes goodnight. It was still not time for the bar to close, and Holmes surveyed who was still left in it.

At another table sat three figures, one woman and two men, two of whom he had met briefly the previous day, and Sherman bravely took up his glass and approached them, asking tentatively if he might join them, to which the woman nodded her head and directed him to an empty chair. 'We met yesterday,' she confirmed.

'That's right. So kind,' he responded. 'I dislike drinking alone.'

'You're welcome, but you don't mind if we talk business, do you?' asked the younger man.

'And you don't have any personal interest in this establishment?' asked the other.

'None whatsoever,' replied Holmes with complete innocence. 'I just feel like a bit of company, that's all.'

Introductions allowed him to meet again Jane Harrison and Niles Carrington, who were fellow guests at the hotel, and Martin Pryke, who was a local solicitor. The three of them immediately restarted their interrupted discussion and Holmes simply leaned back and shamelessly listened.

After a while he began to pick up the threads of their conversation which confirmed what he had learnt the previous day: that Mr Carrington's mother's father was diddled by the Bellamy family over the purchase of the last little building of The Black Swan.

Jane Harrison, he knew, was also involved in a land dispute over ownership, with the late but not so much lamented Berkeley, and it was she who had hooked up with Carrington and called in the solicitor.

In the main, the Bellamy family had been known as ruthless businessmen, not caring who they tangled with or ruined in their dealings, and there were two people who wanted that, not only investigated, but sorted out, hopefully in their favour.

Holmes merely leaned back in his chair and sipped his drink, trying to look totally uninterested in their topic of conversation, while gleefully admitting that here was more grist to the mill.

The party broke up shortly after that, and Holmes went to find out what his new room number was. The ubiquitous Pippa was behind the reception desk, and handed him the keys to room forty-two, assuring him that this was, as his last one had been, a smoking room.

'My dear, I haven't yet had the opportunity to say how awful it must have been to find Ms Maitland like that. And, tell me, will your grandfather's death ruin any plans you had in place for your future, if I may make so bold?'

'My grandfather wanted me to go to college as nobody else in the family did, but I wanted to work towards running the hotel when he decided to retire, and he wasn't getting any younger. To be quite honest, I couldn't be arsed with the idea of another three years of classrooms and teachers, so I was trying to persuade him otherwise, but that doesn't matter now. Somebody's got to run this place, and as I believe I said to you before, I'm going to liven things up.'

'Your work ethic does you credit, young lady,' replied Holmes, before asking how he could find his new room.

Paying careful attention to her instructions, he had no difficulty in finding his way, and put himself to bed to ponder all that he had learnt that day.

After the departure of the constabulary, Garden lay flat on his back in bed, staring at a ceiling that he didn't even acknowledge. The presence of alcohol in his system had made him more perceptive than usual, and it was with great confusion and honesty that he relived his life with his mother since he had left his teens, dismissing the visit of the policemen as unimportant, as he was devoid of any guilt in the matter.

Like countless children before him, he had not really known his mother at all, and had a totally biased and inaccurate impression of how she felt about him. He was willing to acknowledge, having seen her this afternoon chatting in a relaxed manner with Holmes, that she was no scaly monster, and he must have blown things out of all proportion.

How difficult it was to accept that one has been completely wrong over so many years, but he was getting to the stage where there was no doubt that this was what he had done. It would be a long time before he could look at their relationship rationally, but he would do his level best not to lose touch with her, and to approach their conversations with an open mind. He needed to grow up.

His last waking thought was, however, on a totally unrelated subject. This apartment even had gas lighting brackets, something he had only previously heard about from his mother about his great-grandmother's house, which hadn't been updated since the first war, let alone the second. There had been a gas poker in the fireplace, and he wondered if this was for show, too, or whether it was actually still in use. He must ask.

Chapter Nine

Sunday

When Holmes came down for breakfast the next morning, the place was buzzing with news of yet another tragedy, and the police were attending in full force. Heading for the hub of gossip at this time of day: the restaurant part of the bar, he sat down and ordered a pot of Darjeeling and a full breakfast, before enquiring of the waitress what on earth was afoot now.

'It's that Tiffany Jacques. One of the chambermaids went to get fresh linen from the cupboard and, when she opened the door, Tiffany just fell out on top of her. She had hysterics.'

'I'm not surprised. Would that be the linen press near room thirteen?'

'That's the one, sir. She was a right one, was our Tiff, especially where men were concerned. I ran along there when I heard the screaming, and helped lay her body on its back. Well, I don't think I'm telling tales out of school if I say it was obvious she had been wearing loose clothes to try to conceal the fact that she was pregnant. It was just starting to show.'

'Has anybody any idea who the father might be?'

'No one even knew she was up the duff. That's about the only thing she's managed to keep quiet in I don't know how long. Do you want lemon or milk with your tea, sir?'

'Milk, please, and thank you for the information. I wondered what all the fuss was about.'

Garden entered the dining room from an exterior door and sat down opposite him. 'Thank God you're up,' he sighed.

'Why, have you been up long?'

'Just a bit longer than I would have liked to be. They'd only gone and forgotten to move that blasted piper, and it was "Mull of Kintyre" at half past seven. I put the radio on as loud as I could and had a long, hot shower, then I went outside for a couple of cigarettes before coming in to look for you.'

'How are you feeling this morning?'

'Much better, thank you, Holmes. I say, have you heard all this to-do about the maid who was found bolt upright in one of the linen cupboards?'

'The waitress just told me. My mother always said things come in threes.'

At the word 'mother', Garden visibly winced and coloured a bit. 'Sorry, I shouldn't have said that,' Holmes promptly apologised. 'Let's change the subject back to the murders. There have been three now, and I find that rather excessive in such a short time. They must be connected, and it's our job to find out what the common denominator is.' Holmes was sounding determined now.

'When we've eaten, I think. Walls have ears, and a bench outside would probably be the most private we can attain, given the number of people careering round the corridors today,' replied Garden, signalling for the waitress to come and take his order.

Once outside with their respective smokes, Holmes announced a change of plan. 'I believe that, at this stage, there is not enough accurate gossip circulating. The police are the only ones getting the good information, and people are too shocked yet to chatter about things and trivialise events a bit so that they can come to terms with what has happened.

'I suggest that we view the offices again today and perhaps design some advertising and stationery. We will also need a receptionist if we're to have any time to work on cases, and we must give some consideration to the impression we need to make on a public embarrassed about having cause to use our services that will be reassuring but confident. We can't have some flibbertigibbet of a girl. We need a mature woman.'

'Don't you think we'd be better off trying to extract information from people?'

'No, I don't. I think this case is going to be like home-made soup – better if it's left to mature for a couple of days, to allow all the flavours to come out. If we throw ourselves into it too soon, we'll just get hearsay and conjecture. If we wait, some of the truth will, by natural order, bubble to the surface, because people, no matter how hard they try, can't keep things to themselves.'

'But Holmes always said there was no time to lose.'

'Sherlock Holmes was fictional. We are real, and real life is never like fiction. If fiction read like real life, nobody would ever read it – there's too much trivia and time-wasting going on, and too many dead ends.'

'In that case I'll find time to draft a letter of resignation. I can't face going back to working in that office.'

'I think I'll join you in that task, John H. I'm of a like mind, and wish to get on with my new life – our new lives – as quickly as possible. There should be no problem with the lease, and we want to get advertising out into the community as quickly as possible. People may only make a note of our details until they need it, and business may be slow at first, but the sooner we make our presence known, the sooner pens will be noting down our number.'

'When should we go through what we already know? God, I'm so excited. This is the most bizarre thing that has ever happened to me, and I think it's fantastic.'

'Ditto, Garden. I think sometime tomorrow would be a good time to see what we already have, then consider how we're going to extract more information from those who may be involved or may have witnessed something.'

Garden borrowed a tape-measure when they were ready to leave the hotel – being determined to measure up for curtains, etc., Holmes having phoned the agency to ascertain that they could pick up the keys. This being England, almost everywhere *was* open on a Sunday, especially estate agents, car salesrooms, and DIY outlets, catering for when people were free to visit their establishments.

Today, the premises seemed even more suitable. Time had given the layout the opportunity to gel in their minds, and identify itself as perfect for the sort of business they wanted to run, with the bonus of the upstairs flat, not only for accommodation for Garden, but also as extra security. After all, once they were established, the offices would hold files of confidential material on their clients and, hopefully, the presence of somebody in the upstairs flat would deter intruders.

John H. fussed around working out where he could store the respective male and female halves of his wardrobe, and chattered merrily away about how useful his predilection for female attire would be should it be necessary to adopt a disguise for investigations.

Holmes merely nodded. The other man was happy, but he really couldn't foresee a situation where he would be at ease going about in public with his partner dressed as a woman. It was inadvisable, though, to quash such zest and enthusiasm, and he had a feeling time would temper this more to reality.

Although he had never seen John H. dressed in such a manner, Holmes was unsure of his own reaction to such an occurrence, and could not reliably predict what he would look like. It could go either way. He could look just like any other man dressed up as a woman and living a double life – or he could look like his mother. This was a thought that Holmes stifled immediately, as he had by now decided that Mummy Dearest was a very attractive woman, and indeed was already coming to a momentous decision about Mrs Garden.

It was something about which he was currently very uncomfortable putting to his new partner, but the idea refused to go away, and seemed the perfect solution, even if only temporary, to the circumstances in which they currently found themselves. Holmes made little harrumphing noises of discomfort, and got on with drafting his letter of resignation. Time enough the next day to broach what was becoming a very good plan in his own mind.

Garden, meanwhile, carried on with his exciting moving-in plans, his mind a whirl of other thoughts as well, of which only one concerned Holmes' soft spot for his resident cat. Damned great wild animal, he thought, as a vision of Colin, all claws and teeth, entered his mind. He's bigger than a lot of dogs I've known. How could the man be taken in by such a monster?

Maybe the cat really was nervous, and didn't understand that he was actually causing pain? He was sure they'd get used to each other during his temporary occupation of the spare room, and that some sort of truce could be arranged. Garden may have liked animals, but he didn't know them very well.

The other thing that was ringing a tiny bell at the back of his head, making itself heard above the buzz of excitement, was Holmes' eagerness to just abandon their investigation and get on with plans for the office. Surely three murders were more important than desks and chairs? A tiny chill ran through him as he wondered if Holmes was really serious about this whole thing, or if he was just a butterfly that flitted from idea to idea. What if he left his job and Holmes decided to go off on another tangent with his inherited fortune?

No, that couldn't be so. Garden simply wouldn't believe it - but he'd certainly hold off on posting his letter of resignation till he felt a little more certain of their business future together. Finally he convinced himself that Holmes was just as excited as he was and, after all, they hadn't been employed to look into the nefarious deeds at The Black Swan, so if the police solved it first, it was no skin off their noses, although he would, naturally, be very disappointed.

At one point, Garden looked as if he had just had a very good idea, and rushed out of the offices, returning within half an hour with a smile that said the cat had got at the cream again, but gave not a word of explanation to his new partner. They were going to have trouble wheedling information out of people as just themselves. He had just acquired the means for them to do things on a more formal footing. Thank God for Sunday opening hours.

Back in the restaurant for lunch, Holmes began to outline his plans for putting together a more coherent dossier on what they had discovered, and talking about ways of abstracting information when it would seem they had no business to do any such thing.

'Got that one covered, Holmes,' declared Garden with a triumphant grin.

'How?' Holmes was intrigued. If Garden had had a brainwave, why hadn't he himself had it first? After all, he considered himself to be a genius where this detecting lark was concerned: naturally gifted, was how he would describe himself.

Garden slipped a hand into his jacket and extracted a handful of business cards, marked up as representing Holmes and Garden, Private Investigators, and giving the address of the office in the town. 'Here you are, old man.'

'Where on earth did you get these?' asked Holmes in astonishment.

'Stationer's a few doors from the offices. I suddenly remembered that when I'd gone in there once for a newspaper, there had been a card-printing machine near the back: easiest thing in the world to do, to go in and run a few off for our pre-emptive strike on the criminals of this society.'

'How many did you do?'

'Just enough to get us through. We can hand these out and ask away, with most people co-operating without thinking that the offices are not yet open, because that's how life works.'

'By George, I believe you're right.'

They had been late in for lunch and now the crowds of diners had cleared, William Byrd the barman, who had had a very busy shift serving drinks to the local 'roastie' vultures, had just sat down to his own meal.

Rising from his seat, Holmes called the waitress and asked for two coffees, then approached the table where the man sat, just beginning to tuck into his roast pork and apple sauce. 'Mind if we join you?' he asked politely, proffering one of his newly acquired business cards.

Byrd looked at it, at first with suspicion, then with dawning comprehension on his face. 'Thought you two looked like you were in the business,' he commented, and Garden actually winked at Holmes. The magic of an 'official' card was real, and had just proved itself. 'Now, what can I do for you two gentlemen? Personally, I don't have much faith in the plod, but with a professional name like yours, I think I could go along with that.'

Sitting down with a serious expression on his face, Holmes said he wanted to know anything about anyone in the hotel who might have had some sort of grudge against the deceased owner of the hotel. 'After all, we have to start at the beginning, before we can decide whether the three deaths are all down to one person, or whether there are different perpetrators here, and one of the first things we need to know after that, is who definitely has an alibi for any of these foul acts.' He was certainly sounding the part.

Byrd conscientiously worked his way across the contents of his plate with his mind whizzing through what he knew of those who could have had a bone to pick with Bellamy. 'Have you heard anything about that shrinking old violet, Merrilees?' he asked through a mouthful of broccoli.

'Not a word,' Holmes confirmed. 'What have you heard?'

'What I have *over*heard is that she and the old man had a bit of a one-night-stand years ago, and she thought that, as she'd let him pluck her cherry, that he was bound to marry her – silly, naïve bitch. She carried a torch for him for ever after that. That's why she was in tears the other day. The love of her life had gone.'

'By jingo.' Holmes was impressed with this hitherto unexposed piece of information.

'And you know he got that old bat Crumpet pregnant, when she was a gel?'

'Actually, we had heard that,' replied Garden. Thirty-fifteen.

'Righty–ho,' commented Byrd, and gazed at the few scant morsels that remained on his plate, as he once again searched his memory for relevant data. 'There are a couple of guests here who have some sort of beef with the owner – whoever that currently is, although I believe it's that little madam, Pippa – about how certain parts of this establishment were originally purchased, and I believe they are having investigations conducted.'

'You do hear a lot, don't you?' interjected Garden with surprise, as he had already retired the previous evening when Holmes had joined his little after-dinner group, and had temporarily forgotten, in his glee at having a new home, what Holmes had gleaned on Friday evening.

'*Au fait* with that one, Byrd, old boy. Holmes is on the case.'

'Did you know about the guest that the old man screwed a couple of seasons back? Her husband is here snorting fire and brimstone. Think his marriage's gone tits up because of it.'

'Now, that's a new one on me.' Holmes was impressed now. 'Can you recall his name?'

After a short silence, the barman had to admit defeat on this one, but it should be easy enough to ascertain, with the new information 'bombs' that the business cards represented.

'You know about the two old dykes in the guild, don't you?'

'We have come across them, and they don't put up much of a smokescreen if that's their intention.'

'Especially as they live together, and have a cleaner who knows that they share a bedroom. It's bad enough calling themselves Mabs and Lebs, but when they were younger, it used to be Mabsie and Lebsie, and that used to make me want to gag – but it takes all sorts to make a world, and I just let people get on with it,' Byrd concluded generously.

Just as well, thought Garden, as his mind flitted to his large collection of female clothes, and even to the rainbow confection he was wearing today. Without the *laissez-faire* attitude of people like Byrd, his life would be even more of a misery.

'You know Chef hated Bellamy, don't you?' asked the barman, now undoing the belt on his trousers to accommodate the arrival of such a large portion of food.

'He hired a fully trained and qualified man, then fenced him in with seventies stuff and school dinners, and insulted his training and his skills whenever he could. Fair furious was Chef, most of the time, which didn't bother me, because the man's a bully, and he likes to pick on me, so I reckoned he deserved a dose of his own medicine from time to time. Maybe I'll get a bit of a rest, with Pippa letting him have free reign in reconstructing the food here.' There was a look of wistful hope on his face as he said this.

'Could you do us a bit of a favour?' asked Holmes, a look of hope on his face.

'If I can. Anything to bring a killer, or killers, to justice.'

'Could you have a bit of a think about who might have been under your steady gaze when things actually happened, so that we can eliminate certain people from our enquiries?'

'Course I can. I'll put me mind to it during me afternoon break. I've got a notepad at the back of the bar for orders, so I'll just scribble some thoughts on that while I wait for my next shift.'

The two newly minted investigators suddenly realised that they had missed lunch in their absorption with the current situation, and hastily ordered sandwiches to see them through to the evening meal.

Later, in the residents' lounge, Holmes decided that after Garden's brainwave in printing some cards and their informative little chat with the barman, they could probably do with having a round-up now of what they knew, so that they could decide what they now needed to know, as far as this was possible to anticipate.

'I'm getting damned suspicious about that Ladies' Guild,' he began. 'The Maitland woman was almost leaning over my shoulder when poor old Bellamy went out of the window. What if it was her who pushed him, and she just had time to skip out of the way as he teetered on the brink?'

'Well, it didn't do her a lot of good, did it? She was the next victim.' Garden was not so enthusiastic. 'So she couldn't have had anything to do with the other two, could she?'

'Fair enough, but there might have been someone else hanging around that I just didn't see, and La Maitland did. They were all in that little room, you know. Who knows who might have slipped out for a minute to powder their nose or pitch a man through an upstairs window? And the woman herself could have done it, then been seen, and been knocked off herself. We could have a couple of killers on our hands, as well as whichever one of them killed the poor maid.'

'True.' Garden suddenly became thoughtful. 'And La Maitland was at another of their committee meetings when she met her end. There could easily be a tie-in there. We're going to have to hunt them down one by one and give them a bit of a grilling, but how on earth are we going to get their addresses?'

'Elementary, my dear Garden. Ladies like that would be more likely to have a landline telephone than a mobile, so I suggest we just go through the local telephone directory. I can't see anyone from that little mob wanting the anonymity of ex-directory listing, can you? Or having just a mobile phone?'

'Sneaky old Holmes. Of course! The answer was right under my nose and I couldn't see it. I can understand how Watson felt now.' Garden's mood was a mixture of contrite and excited. 'What do you think of all the legal stuff about irregular purchasing of parts of the property?'

'I think that can wait for now, and I'll schmooze the solicitor – for I discovered who was handling the business last night after you retired – and see if I can get a little dirt from him as to how likely it is that that outcome will be to the detriment of the current situation.'

'We seem, on reflection, what with one-night-stands,

crushes, abortions, and what not, to have got quite a lot of grist for our mill. Do you think there's more out there?' Garden wasn't good with new situations, and needed to know what his Mummy Dearest used to call 'the ins and outs of a duck's arse', before he would accept anything.

'Got to be, old boy. What we've got is probably just the tip of the iceberg: loads of intrigue in the undercurrents of small-town life. We are now part of that, and must become expert at sorting the wheat from the chaff.'

'I say, Holmes.'

'Yes?'

'You haven't swallowed a book of clichés, have you?'

'Shut up, you ignorant young pup, or I shall throw you outside with no supper.' Garden just grinned. This was a new situation he thought he could very soon grow used to: so much better than just inhabiting an office chair all day and shuffling papers from one pile to the next.

After a full and slightly celebratory dinner to mark their unofficial launch into the detection business, they spent the evening in Holmes' room making a decent dossier on their current findings, and going through the local telephone directory to avail themselves of the home addresses of the Ladies' Guild committee members. They were on their way now.

Chapter Ten

Monday

Over breakfast, Holmes and Garden had discussed tactics, and decided just to turn up at the addresses they had garnered. Surprise was the best weapon, they considered, as they were hoping to get the women of the guild to spill some information that they were trying to conceal. Office fitments temporarily forgotten, Holmes was back on the case wholeheartedly, much to Garden's relief.

They had got a local town map from Reception on their way to breakfast, and got egg yolk and brown sauce all over it working out their best and most efficient route. 'If we go to the left on leaving the hotel,' began Holmes, plonking a sticky finger on to the representation of The Black Swan, 'we can make our first call on Millicent Fitch at Tall Trees, which the directory reliably informs me is in River Road, here, just behind the shops.

'Then, if we return to the main shopping street, we can go up Tupps Alley where we will find Anna Merrilees at Moon Cottage, at number twenty-seven. If we then cross over to the other side of the main street, we can have a look at the outside of La Maitland's house at Hunters View, 31 Drubbs Lane. Sorry about reciting all these addresses, but I find it easier to remember something if I've said it out loud.

'After that,' continued the older man, his finger on the move again, his moustache quivering with excitement, 'we can visit Agatha Crumpet at The Hedges, 18 Hedging Cut, and, finally, on to Marion Guest and Lesley Piper at Freesia Cottage, situation, 18 Puddle Path.'

'You seem to have got that all worked out,' said Garden, slightly impressed, even though he had resisted the feeling. 'How long do you think this is going to take us?'

'Absolutely no idea, old boy. Never done this sort of thing before, so we'll just have to play it by ear,' he replied, shattering the illusion of having everything under control that his previous speech had engendered. 'We'll just take things as they come. In the main though, I think I should lead the questioning, and you should endeavour to pick up as much stuff visually as you can. Can learn a lot about someone by the place they live and the way they furnish and decorate it.'

Folding the map, Holmes made ready to be off, and Garden wiped his mouth prissily on a napkin and rose too. 'We'll amalgamate what we've learnt at the end of this exercise, then?' he asked, in clarification.

'Absolutely. I'm sure, between us, we can work out a decent modus operandi in this business.' Holmes was sounding a little more confident than he felt, because he was just as at sea as Garden was, but was bolstering himself up with false confidence, because he didn't want to cramp the style of his dream, and let it languish, rather than flourish. This had to work, didn't it?

On their way out, there were noises of anger and distress coming from the reception desk, where they espied young Pippa deep in a hushed conversation with one of the female guests. 'I don't know whether the woman's complaining about something, but she'd got Pippa all fired up,' commented Garden.

'Yes, but no time to probe now. We'll see what we can find out later,' decided Holmes, dismissively. The final thing they heard was the young owner's voice raised in a yell of, 'Over my dead body.'

The town was not busy even though the tourist season was approaching fast, and River Road was easy to find, being the first turning to the left off the main shopping street. Tall Trees wasn't far from the main drag, and proved to be an old cottage that had been renovated to within an inch of its life. There was more of Disney than of olde worlde charm about it, and the final vestiges of this charm had gone with the external decoration, so black and white as to be untrue, with some of the beams obvious fakes.

Although this could easily have been a nod to The Black Swan, it just looked like the owner suffered from OCD, and couldn't bear even a blade of grass out of place. Every brick in the chimneys had new pointing, and the garden would not have disgraced a miniature park.

'So this is where the woman lives who had a one-nighter with old Bellamy?' asked Garden, just to get things straight in his mind, almost simultaneously with the door being opened by a tiny bird-like woman, almost continental in her immaculate turn-out. Her hair was grey and well-cut, her light make-up precisely suited to her years and colouring. Even at this time, on a normal Monday morning, when she had probably been expecting no visitors, she was immaculately turned out in a light grey skirt suit over a soft ivory blouse, and looked quite the Saga fashion-plate. She had absolutely nothing in common with the average English countrywoman.

'Good morning. Miss Fitch, I presume,' stated Holmes, holding out one of their recently acquired business cards. 'I wonder if we might have a word with you about the trouble at the hotel.' This was an understatement, but one that was appreciated by the precise spinster, but she wasn't as green as she was cabbage-looking.

'May I ask on whose behalf you are working? Exactly who has asked you to look into this?' she asked, an intelligent light behind her eyes.

'You may well ask,' blustered Holmes, as Garden's

shoulders slumped. Clocked and dismissed so soon? 'However,' his partner continued, 'we are not able to reveal our client's personal details for reasons of professional integrity. I'm sure you can understand how a client may not want it to be generally known that he, or she, is pursuing certain information until that information has been gathered.'

Nice work, thought Garden, as the woman's face cleared, and she seemed to accept this transparent excuse without question. Confidentiality was something almost everyone craved these days, especially with the intrusiveness of CCTV, general security cameras, and even the eyes of spy satellites and online map-makers.

Miss Fitch ushered them into a preternaturally clean and tidy sitting room furnished in the antique style so beloved of the 1980s, and bade them plant their bottoms on little chintz sofas, of which there were three in the room.

'May I offer you any refreshment?' she asked politely and, when they refused, sat on the third and only vacant sofa. 'So, how can I help you?' she next enquired, a little intrigued to be visited by such an exotic species as a pair of private investigators.

Clearing his throat to bolster his confidence, Holmes began. 'First, we would like to know how well you knew Mr Berkeley Bellamy.' This seemingly innocent question caused Miss Fitch to blush a deep crimson and look away.

'I knew him quite well some time ago,' she managed, almost in a whisper, unable to look either of her visitors in the eye.

'You were, in fact, intimate with him?' Holmes said this almost sadistically.

'I was, but I don't want that bandied about, gentlemen. I'm really not that sort of person. I was once very fond of him, however.'

'Thank you for your honestly,' Holmes rewarded her,

with a return to his avuncular manner. 'And may I ask where you were when the unfortunate gentleman met his death?'

Miss Fitch cringed at such blunt language and finally admitted that she was in the 'small room' at the hotel where the committee meeting had been taking place.

'And you didn't leave that room?'

'Only to – wash my hands,' she replied, with a return to embarrassment.

'And where were you when Margery Maitland was murdered?' Time for some strong meat again.

'I was in the room waiting for Margery to return with the refreshment trolley. Unfortunately poor Pippa couldn't spare us any waitress staff that time.'

'And did you leave the room?' The question was repeated with unnecessary emphasis on the second word.

'To powder my nose,' the woman replied, barely audible above the buzz of guilt in her head. 'But I didn't touch either of them.'

'And what about Tiffany Jakes? What do you know about her demise, and where were you at the time it happened?' But this time Holmes had overstepped the mark. Not only did the woman they were questioning not know the exact time the woman had been murdered, but neither did they, so a stalemate ensued.

In a final attempt to extract something, Holmes went for pot black. 'Is it not true that you were insanely jealous of Miss Jakes, because she was carrying your ex-lover's child, and you had never had that honour?'

She didn't exactly beat Holmes about the head with the *Radio Times*, but she certainly hooshed them out of the house *tout de suite*, and slammed the door on them, leaving them in no doubt as to the state of her temper.

Holmes was left leaning up against the front wall, where he had hurtled under the pursuit of a very angry elderly lady, and Garden sauntered up to him and said,

'Pushed it a bit far there, didn't you?'

'Fortune favours the brave,' replied Holmes, trying to regain his dignity. He'd been well and truly ousted and reminded that, like everyone else, he had feet of clay, and couldn't get away with murder, even if someone at the hotel thought that they could.

'But not the foolhardy. Come along, Holmes old man: suspects to question, investigations to undertake.' Holmes' run-in had given Garden new confidence, and he thought he might get in a bit of the questioning on their next visit. It was all very well to tell him to count frills and furbelows, but it was his investigation too. 'You came down pretty hard on her.'

'As a shot in the dark, it certainly raised a cry of distress,' his partner replied, suddenly rather pleased with the reaction he had provoked. 'It's certainly food for thought. With a house like that, the old dear's as repressed as they come. No telling what she might have done if provoked.'

'But she was in tears afterwards,' tempered Garden.

'Of the crocodile variety, my friend. Just camouflage. Crackin' stuff! Onwards and upwards,' he carolled, rubbing his hands together in complete recovery. A rubber ball had nothing on Holmes.

The route to Tupps Lane was an easy one, initially taking them back to the main street, where Holmes admitted he had to go and stock up on pipe tobacco. Charging Holmes with the task of getting him some more cigarettes, Garden went off on a mission of his own, and they met ten minutes later at the entrance to the lane. 'What have you been up to?' asked Holmes, mildly annoyed that Garden had used him like an errand boy while he took care of something as yet undisclosed.

'Went back to get a couple more small batches of those business cards. Thought we might need them if this is what we're going to be doing,' he replied, to receive a grin of approval.

'Good thinking, my boy. Just what we need to further our investigations, if the last visit's anything to go by.'

Moon Cottage was part of a terrace that once must have been a farm labourer's dwelling, and was what an estate agent would have described as bijou – barely big enough to swing a cat, in in common parlance.

The owner of this 'jewel' answered the door like a refugee from a rather bohemian colony, wearing a plethora of beads and scarves, her hair long and loose about her shoulders. She had looked nothing like this when they had come across her at the hotel, and the two men both decided that she had a secret persona at home.

Bangles positively jangled as she waved an arm to admit them, and she had sandals that laced to halfway up her calves, under a rather floaty frocky kaftan-like garment. Her scent was musky, her eyes hopeful. 'What can I do for you gentlemen?' she almost breathed, in an effort, perhaps, to sound sexy.

'Holmes beamed at her and handed her one of the now-so-useful business cards. Her eyes widened, she looked up under lowered lashes to say, 'Private investigators – how exciting. This is quite an adventure for me. Can I get you anything while we talk? I'm sure you're here about what has been happening at The Black Swan. Shocking!'

The way she said the last word was almost salacious. The woman was actually getting a kick out of the situation. How arid her existence must be, and how rooted in fantasy, if she looked like that and had as yet trapped no mate.

As they settled into feathery, plump armchairs, Miss Merrilees, for such was she, wafted round the room lighting incense sticks and cones. 'So necessary to create the right atmosphere,' she commented, lavishing a smile on them. Holmes looked a trifle flustered to have arrived so unexpectedly in an ashram, but Garden had a small smile on his face as he admired the woman's sheer style.

Before Holmes could gather his resources, she had begun the conversation for him. 'So tragic about poor Bellamy. I had such a soft spot for him. All he really needed was the love of a good woman, and he would have been reformed.' Here, she sighed. 'It's not as if I didn't try, though I never bruited my feelings abroad, but he wasn't the sort of man who surrenders easily. You can lead a horse to water, but that's about as far as I ever got. Drink, I could not make it.'

'That's very candid of you, Miss Merrilees,' said Garden, busily taking notes in his tiny notebook. If they were touting themselves as official, there was no reason at all that he couldn't look official and actually make a note of what was being disclosed to them.

Regarding Holmes' still astounded face, she gave a throaty chuckle, and explained, 'My life outside this house is everything the life of a woman of my age and social standing should be – hence the Ladies' Guild membership. But here, in my own tiny paradise, I live a life more exciting. I can be a *femme fatale* in my own home whereas, in public, I'd just attract ridicule.

'I don't go out much, for my life is here, reading romantic stories and making them up. I actually write now and again for a ladies' magazine under a pen-name and, I suppose, I have become rather bohemian in my introverted little world.

'Maybe you've even heard of my alter ego, for I've just begun to write for Bills and Moon, the romantic publishers. I am Dolores Dalrymple,' she stated, with a flourish of a trailing scarf, then proceeded to fit a cigarette into a long holder and look around for a lighter. 'Purely herbal,' she explained, inviting them to light up if they pleased.

Holmes, who had been wondering what the strange

smell of bonfire was inside the cottage, got his pipe out as if on automatic pilot. This, he had not expected at all, to find such a hot-house flower behind the door of this tiny dwelling: one who had masqueraded before as an everyday middle-aged to elderly woman.

Garden was quicker, and was already puffing happily away on a Superking. 'Did you and Mr Bellamy get on well?' he asked, thinking it was time that they got down to business.

'Perfectly well, provided I didn't crowd him. I think I made him nervous. He had been round here for supper once, and I think my indoor personality intimidated him.' Not surprising, thought Garden. It seems to have done the same to Holmes.

'You didn't kill him for spurning you, then?' asked the, until-now-silent partner, then blushed at his own clumsiness. Instead of ejecting him bodily from her home, Anna Merrilees let loose a fruity chuckle, and replied, 'If I'd ever attacked dear old Berkeley, I'd be much more likely to ravish him than kill him. Silly man!'

Holmes had had enough, and rose, with some difficulty, from his feathery perch. Anna Merrilees went over to offer him a hand, but he waved her away warily, and headed for the door like a dog that needs to go out urgently to do its business. It was Garden who stayed behind to thank her for her time, and to emerge, finally, into fresh air, trying to cough the clouds of incense smoke from his lungs which were quite happy with cigarette smoke, thank you very much.

Once more, Garden found his partner at a loss, leaning in a lack-lustre manner against the tiny porch. 'Scary woman,' breathed Holmes, removing a handkerchief from his breast pocket and wiping his forehead, 'I can see her wiping out a reluctant lover without a second thought – almost like swatting a fly.'

'I thought her individual style was rather magnificent,

considering how well she covers up her private life. I might even have a look at some of her writing.'

'Stuff and nonsense! Come on, let's get on to the next one, before I lose my nerve.' It was a much-chastened Holmes who had emerged from their first two skirmishes into private investigation.

Their next house call was one that held no fears, as it was just to look at the exterior of where the Ladies' Guild's head honchette, the recently deceased Margery Maitland, had lived. She had resided across on the other side of the main retail centre of the small town, and Hunters View in Drubbs Lane proved to be a large four-square Victorian dwelling in fair order, considering that there was so much maintenance for just one person to keep a rein on.

It looked rather like the woman had herself. It presented a very respectable front, and was quite bulky, with a slightly forbidding cast to its frontage due to the presence of so much evergreen shrubbery. It did not appear to have a large garden, but the presence of a fairly new bungalow on each side of it spoke of land sold off to help with the upkeep.

'Big place for a woman on her own to live. She did live on her own, didn't she?' asked Garden.

'Indubitably. I asked the barman. He seems to have a bit of gen on all their regulars. Part of the job, I suppose, just picking up the odd titbit of information and storing it away in case it ever proved useful. It did in my case, because I stayed on for an extra couple of drinks on the strength of his info.'

'So, why exactly are we here?' Garden was just a little confused. 'I know you found her at your shoulder when old man Bellamy went out of the window, but she was the next victim, so it couldn't be her who was responsible for the three deaths.'

'Very true, but she could have done the first one, as we

discussed before, and been seen, that person finishing off not just her but maybe the pregnant girl as well. We need to establish who saw what. We could have two murderers here, or it could be that dear old Margery – I don't think – saw something at the first murder, and the murderer was seen again when he did away with her.'

'So, we could still be looking for one or several murderers, then?'

'Precisely.'

'What do you think about the two women we've spoken to so far?'

'Could be either of them. They're both very suspicious.'

'Do you think so?'

'Oh, yes.'

'So you've not eliminated either of them?'

'Not to my mind. Both dead suspicious.'

Garden couldn't see it himself, but left his new friend to his musings, and just thought about who lived in a house like this. 'Did you get any more from your barman?' he asked.

'Just that old Margery detested Berkeley Bellamy, and thought he had the town in much too tight a grip for a man with no class.'

'She was jealous of his standing in the local community?'

'Green as a pea. Byrd said she reckoned to have better breeding, and that she should hold some of the honorary and official positions that had been conveyed on him.'

'Good motive?'

'Very good motive. That means that we're looking for someone else as well, though.'

'Jolly dee!' Garden wasn't impressed. Surely Holmes was over-complicating things. Only time would tell.

A call on Agatha Crumpet at The Hedges in Hedging Cut

took them on their return journey towards The Black Swan, and marked the beginning of the second half of the task they had set themselves for the day. Both of them were in awe of this formidable woman since they had discovered that Bellamy had impregnated her and caused her to seek what was then the very shameful act of abortion.

The woman who answered the door of what appeared to be a knocked-through group of three cottages was dressed in an apron, and held a feather duster in her hand. She was no comedy French maid, however, but a redoubtable matron who had seen at least six decades of her life slip into the past.

'We would like to speak to Ms Agatha Crumpet, if you would be so kind,' asked Holmes, with his most winsome smile, his confidence back on the up.

'Miss Crumpet is not receiving visitors at the moment,' came back the implacable reply.

'I'm sure she'll see us,' countered Holmes, and smiled again, this time with a tiny strain at the edges.

'Madam is not receiving this afternoon,' said this sturdy domestic, and began to close the door.

Garden's foot was over the jamb like lightning, and he held out one of the new cards he had had printed that morning.

'I'm sure Ms Crumpet will see us when you present our visiting card,' he informed her in a business-like manner. He'd been bullied enough in his life, in his opinion, by a woman, and he wasn't going to take any ess-aitch-eye-tee from this old maid.

'Wait here,' she snapped, and put the security chain on the door. 'I'll ask her.'

It was the formidable figure of Agatha Crumpet herself who returned to let them in. 'You must excuse Winnie,' she boomed. 'I've given her very strict instructions that I'm not to be disturbed in the afternoons. She thinks it's because I'm writing Daddy's memoirs, but, to be honest, it's the only way I can get some peace for my afternoon nap.'

This was a not-inauspicious start, and they followed her into what she described as the drawing room. It was indeed finely decorated, and included some first-class pieces of Georgian furniture and ornamentation.

'I take it you're here about that dreadful business up at The Black Swan – there's nothing else going on around here at the moment of which I'm aware.'

'That's right – may I call you Agatha?' Holmes was going in for a softer approach this time.

'You may certainly not. We hardly know each other. You may call me Miss Crumpet and be done with. And I shall address you as …' Here, she looked down at the card which she still held in her hand. 'Mr Holmes or Mr Garden?' she continued. 'What extraordinary names. Why can't you be Holmes and Watson?'

There was no answer to this, so Holmes stood, and held out his hand, mumbling, 'Sherman Holmes at your service, Miss Crumpet. Delighted to meet you.'

'John H. Garden, Miss Crumpet.' Garden followed suit, then left it to his partner to get the conversational ball rolling. Before this could happen, however, Holmes' face took on a greenish tinge, and he held his handkerchief to his mouth as if he were feeling sick. Garden looked at him in bewilderment, then he caught it, too. The whiff of a rich and fruity fart was slowly engulfing both of them, although Holmes seemed to have got the worst of it. Surely the woman hadn't dropped one in front of new acquaintances?

Agatha Crumpet didn't turn a hair, and asked them if they would like to get on with their business, as she had an interrupted appointment with Morpheus to finish. Holmes rose and walked to the window, where he leaned on the sill and gasped for air, rather like a fish out of water.

'Whatever is the matter, Mr Holmes?' his hostess asked, puzzled, but the miasma must have finally reached her, and she fluffed a hand in front of her face. 'Come out from under there, Fudge. It's no good pretending you're not there, for you've given away your presence in your normal, disgusting manner.

'I'm sorry gentlemen, but my little doggie has a bit of a digestive problem in his old age, and I normally manage to keep him out of this room.'

Rising to shoo the animal from beneath Holmes' former perch, she shut the door on him, reached behind a Staffordshire figure on the mantelpiece, and sprayed generously with an aerosol room freshener. 'That should do it. Please do take a seat again, Mr Holmes.'

One look at Holmes' queasy countenance changed her mind, however. 'I think we'll retire to the conservatory where the air is a little clearer, and we can start all over again. Do accept my apologies. Little chap has been banned from Ladies' Guild meetings for the last six months or so.'

When Winnie had staggered in with an enormous tray containing a silver tea service and some fine bone china, Holmes had recovered sufficiently to advise their hostess that they were here for details of a rather personal and embarrassing incident in her past.

'I suppose someone has blabbed about my termination,' she replied, confrontationally.

'That is the subject to which I was referring.'

'Than call a spade a bloody spade, man. But I'll tell you now, I don't talk about that – ever. It happened. You've evidently found out about it. It was unfortunate. The end. I'll leave you to finish your tea in peace, then I want you to leave my house, and never return. I have nothing further to say to you on this subject or any other.'

With that, she grabbed her cup and left the glassed area, a look of determination on her face and a stiffness in her ramrod straight back which broached no rebuke.

'That's us kicked in the balls again,' sighed Garden.

'What did you just say?' asked Holmes, hoping that he had not heard right.

'I just said that that didn't go very well,' lied Garden, his fingers crossed under his saucer.

Chapter Eleven

Still Monday

Their last visit of the day was the one that had intrigued them most about their task, being to the residence of two lesbians – and everyone knows how silly men can be about lesbians of whatever age group.

In Freesia Cottage, down the intriguingly named Puddle Path, they found what looked very like the cover of a giant chocolate box. A thatched property with a stone boundary wall to its land sat amidst the perfect English cottage garden. Every plant that should have been blooming was, and a few more besides, the names of which neither of them knew. In the centre of one half of the front lawn stood a stone bird-bath and in the absolute centre of the other half sat a sundial.

'Good Lord, Holmes,' exclaimed Garden. 'I thought we were about Conan Doyle, but we seemed to have strayed on to the set for an Agatha Christie story here.'

'It's almost too picture-perfect to be true,' agreed Holmes. 'Check your watch and ascertain we haven't travelled back to the 1920s, will you?'

'I wonder if the inside matches?' wondered Garden out loud, as his partner manipulated the brass lion door knocker.

Both women appeared at the door, and Garden assumed that they had been a partnership for some time. Just as some married couples grew to look like each other over decades of mirroring each other's expressions, so these two women would have been difficult to identify individually if encountered separately.

Both had beige-coloured hair – with more than a little help to nature – and a light wave, the tresses styled short but soft. Both were of a similar height and build, and wore not-quite-matching frocks that had obviously been made for them – same material, slightly different styles. It felt to both men as if they had slightly cock-eyed double vision, and both blinked in surprise.

The pair had not appeared so similar in public, so maybe this appearance of duality was something only indulged in in private. Holmes' thoughts went even further, and he wondered if maybe they didn't have a decent full-length mirror, so simply used each other for the purposes of checking their appearance.

Mabs Guest – as the first lady introduced herself, commenting that they had already met at the hotel – had on slightly brighter lipstick than her partner and, therefore, offered a distinguishing feature with which to tell the women apart. Lebs Piper also entered the fun of who was who by having on slightly more dangly earrings, and so they were invited inside.

The interior of the property caused them both some surprise. Here was femininity gone mad. Just about everything in the place was be-frilled or covered in lace with the exception of the beams, and everything not thus decorated was adorned with objects that fitted these criteria. Even the wall-lampshades – for the ceiling was too low for ceiling light-fittings – were covered in lacy little frills.

The predominant colours were a sort of dusky pink and a dull baby blue, and it was rather like being smothered, being ushered into shapeless old armchairs. Holmes had already given each of them one of the business cards and both, at the same time, reached for pairs of spectacles which hung about their necks on chains.

'I expect you've come about all the murder and mayhem at The Black Swan,' mooted Mabs mischievously, evidently the slightly more outgoing of the pair. 'Absolutely dreadful.'

'Disgraceful!' added Lebs, giving both men a penetrating gaze. 'And who has asked you to work on these unhappy events?' she asked astutely.

'Madam, confidentiality forbids that we should discuss our client, or clients, in any of our cases. Please, rest assured, however, that justice is our only aim.'

Lebs gave them a look that said she hadn't been taken in at all. 'It's that little tart, Pippa, isn't it? Not content with netting the whole kit and caboodle, she's going for the murderer to bring a private case for compensation for loss of business, I'll bet.'

'How can you say that about the poor girl?' asked Mabs suddenly showing a soft-hearted side.

'Well, you would say that, wouldn't you? All you're after is a quick fumble with her ripe young body.'

'How dare you!'

'I dare, because it's true. You're just dying to get your hands on some young meat.'

'Who could blame me, with a scrawny old cow like you being the only thing on offer in my life?'

'That's not what you used to say in bed,' Lebs confronted her partner.

'That's because, as I said before, I was thinking of Pippa instead of boring old – yes, old – you. And you *are* old, you can't deny the fact.'

'And so are *you.*'

Holmes was on his feet, waving his arms about to attract attention.

Mabs yelled at Lebs, ignoring his semaphore. 'I never used to say a word when you almost went straight, and started mooning about her grandfather shortly after we first got together.'

'You knew about that?'

'How could I not have guessed? You were like a dying duck in a thunderstorm for months on end.'

'We'll be off then. This is something that you would, no doubt, prefer to sort out in private, I'm sure,' Holmes almost shouted. Garden rose and went with him to the door. 'Good afternoon, er, ladies,' Holmes called.

'Thank you for your help,' Garden lied. There really was nothing else he could think of to say.

The squabble had blown up like a summer squall, and Holmes did his best to quash it before it got to the hair-pulling and face-scratching stage. 'Ladies! Ladies! I understand you're upset about what has happened, but falling out about it won't solve anything.'

'What do you know, you stupid man?' Lebs was on the attack. 'I'm just about sick and tired of this silly old dyke mooning about her beloved Pippa, with never a thought for the one who shops, cooks, and launders for her. Where am I in this equation? Nowhere. Well, I might just up sticks and leave you to your beloved Pippa.'

'Lebs!'

'If you made any approach to her, I'm sure she'd vomit on the spot and bar you for life.'

Back in the hotel, both men adjourned to their own rooms for a rest, neither of them having uttered more than a few words on the short walk back to their accommodation. They were both too shocked at the fall-out between the two women, most prominently because of their age, and the fact that the subject was a sexual one. A fall-out about the garden or décor they could have coped with, but sexuality and all that implied had left the pair of them, both rather conservative characters underneath, severely disconcerted.

When Holmes came downstairs, about an hour or so before he planned to eat, he made straight for the bar to get himself a snifter to steady himself after all the events of their investigations earlier.

Carrying his glass over to an armchair with good view of the door, he noticed in a corner on the other side of the room the figure of a woman. Although she was slightly in shadow, he knew instantly that she wasn't a guest he had encountered before, and she gave the appearance of being rather attractive.

At first he was embarrassed when she noticed that he was looking in her direction, and looked away, only to catch, out of the corner of his eye, the fact that she was wiggling the fingers of one hand at him in greeting – almost in invitation.

Now, Holmes had led an emotionally stunted life, and had had very little to do with what he occasionally referred to as 'the fairer sex', and he could feel the heat of the blush that rose in his cheeks, and looked away again, sinking his face into his glass to cover his embarrassment.

A minute or two later, he sneaked another look at this enigmatic woman and, once again, she raised her fingers in a small gesture of greeting. This time, emboldened slightly by his alcoholic beverage, he raised a single finger in reply, and went to the bar to purchase a refill. As he waited for William Byrd to furnish him with his order, he glanced sideways in the direction of this intriguing stranger again.

She certainly looked attractive, he decided, his eyes having become used to the lower light level in the bar by now. Was he about to be involved in a little interlude of intrigue, he wondered uncharacteristically? Clutching his glass, he returned to his seat, and pondered what appeared to be an unexpected opportunity in his life.

Keeping his gaze determinedly away from this siren, he risked another longer stare when she went to the bar and bought herself another glass of wine, noticing the easy glide with which she moved. Holmes would never have described himself as a romantic soul, but he could feel the stirrings of such an emotion inside him right now.

When he was almost ready to go through for his meal, wondering vaguely when his partner was going to come down, and rather hoping that he wouldn't, he risked another look in the woman's direction and, once again, she signalled a slight wiggle of her fingers. By George, he was going to ask her if she would take dinner with him this evening.

As he contemplated this move, however, his quarry drained her glass and stood, preparatory to leaving the bar area but, instead of heading straight for the door, she veered in his direction and moved slowly and seductively towards him. By golly, this looked promising.

As she reached his table, she leaned low into his ear, and a very familiar voice whispered, 'Gotcha, didn't I, old man?'

Chapter Twelve

Tuesday

Holmes could barely contain his embarrassment the previous evening, had gone to his room to eat there in solitary confinement, and had woken up on Tuesday morning, his mind split in two. One half cringed away from the thought that he had been completely taken in by John H., and had even found his female persona attractive. The other half roiled like the waves of an angry storm-tossed sea.

With such a versatile partner, it would be like working with two completely different people, so far as the outside world was concerned, and the possibilities of what they might be able to get away with were almost endless, although he couldn't see as far as Garden actually attending a meeting of the Ladies' Guild and getting away with it without being rumbled.

At breakfast the next morning, he could barely contain his discomfort as he watched what a small part of him considered the hermaphrodite Garden enter the room and approach the table, but Garden acted as if nothing untoward had happened and, not being a mind-reader, he had no idea about his partner's delicate and unusual feelings towards the figure he had presented the previous evening.

He merely said, 'I am rather good, aren't I? I bet you thought I'd look like a drag queen in my female gear.' Holmes gulped, and nodded silent agreement. 'I think I do a convincingly good job though. I bet you couldn't tell me from the real thing, and to be quite honest, I have had a pass made at me a few times, but I'd hate to give some poor unsuspecting man a heart attack, even in the name of innocent fun.'

Holmes swallowed noisily and nodded again. 'Er, um, yes, very good indeed. Well done, old boy.'

'Think how useful I could be going undercover in some of our future cases. Everyone will know you have a male partner, so I could be a real secret weapon.'

That made Holmes sit up straight in his rather uncomfortable chair. 'What a thought! We'd be a really unique Holmesian duo, wouldn't we? Holmes and the cross-dressing Garden. Watson was never so interesting.' In the excitement of the possibilities of this side of his new partner, Holmes had completely forgotten his discomfiture at what had taken place the previous evening, and was looking forward to many occasions when he could send Garden into situations in which he himself would stand out like a sore thumb.

'We'd have to keep me under wraps, as it were,' replied John H., 'but I don't think I'd like to bruit abroad such a delicate flower in the confines of this small town,' he replied. 'To date I've usually done this in complete privacy. Apart from investigations, I think I'd like to come out gradually, and still keep my other self under wraps.'

'Suits me down to the ground, John H. Secret weapons work much better when they are kept just that – secret.'

'But you'd never be at a loss for a partner if we ever had to go to a function together.' That gave Holmes pause for thought. 'You could always describe me as one of your distant cousins. I mean, people must know, if they know about your inheritance, that you have far-flung relatives.'

That made Holmes feel much better. If he could describe the 'woman' on his arm as a distant cousin, it wouldn't feel so damned weird, knowing it was not only a man, but his business partner. 'I think you may be on to something there. You and your frocks and make-up might be the secret of our future success, as long as mum's the word.'

'As long as it's not my mum, I don't mind at all,' said Garden, giving a rueful smile at this sideways reference to Mummy Dearest. 'So, do we have a round-up of what we learnt yesterday after breakfast, then decide on the plan for today?'

'Right on, Garden,' agreed Holmes, being more right on than he realised.

'And just where did you get the clothes and make-up for yesterday's little stunt?' the older man surprised himself by asking.

'I sort of picked them up when we went round to my old address. My, but it felt good to put on my other skin and be somebody else again. Haven't done that for a while.'

'Well, please warn me when you're going to be doing it again,' requested Holmes, looking down ruefully at the splotch of egg yolk on his shirt front. He had never been a messy eater, but today was different, and his appetite had diminished with the mental state in which he found himself.

Garden was also similarly in a heightened mental state. He had been so slapdash taking off his make-up the night before that he had woken this morning with decidedly panda-like eyes, but Holmes didn't notice anything amiss. He had a few points about which he was still curious, and now cleared his throat preparatory to enquiring.

'Hrmph! There are a few things I'm quite curious about, but I shall understand perfectly if you're a little chary of answering them,' he began.

Garden gave him a wary glance, and told him to go ahead. He'd answer as best as he could.

'Well, what do you do with your, um, er … your, ah,

undercarriage?' Holmes blushed furiously on the last word of this question, and cast his eyes down towards the tabletop, not wishing to look Garden in the eye in case he had caused him undue embarrassment.

'That's an easy one,' Garden answered with ease. 'Everything just tucks up inside, out of the way. There's a sort of cavity. I first learnt about it when I saw an interview with the drag queen Danny la Rue, and I find it gives a much more realistic outline in trousers.'

'Jolly good. Jolly good,' replied Holmes, and cleared his throat loudly again. 'And what about your, um, Adam's apple? That's very difficult to disguise, isn't it? Nowhere to tuck that, eh?'

'No, but I always wear a scarf round my neck. You probably didn't notice last night, but I had one on then. Not only is it a stylish touch of colour, but it covers the offending article, so that no attention is brought to it.'

'Ingenious, old chap. And the stubble? I didn't see a hint of five o'clock shadow when I, er, saw you last night.'

'A very close shave with a wet razor normally does the trick. But, mind, it has to be very close, but careful as well. I can't go around wearing make-up with little cuts all over my face, now can I?'

'Not at all. Well, how, er, fascinating. Thank you for sharing your little tricks with me.'

'Not at all. If you ever fancy finding out what your feminine side looks like, just let me know, and we can do something with a loose shift and make-up bag, plus a suitable wig.'

'Thanks for the offer, but I think I'll pass for now,' Holmes replied, suddenly feeling slightly nauseous at the thought of being in full female rig, with warpaint and false hair to boot. There was no way on God's earth that he was ever going to try that!

Garden had left his cigarettes upstairs and, as Holmes

strolled outside for an after-breakfast pipe, he trailed off, once more in search of where they had put his room this morning. On his rather roundabout route, he once again came across the little boot cupboard, and could hear sounds of distress coming from inside.

Being a soft-hearted man, he knocked discreetly on the door and opened it a crack to peek in to see if he could be of any assistance. Inside was Pippa Berkeley, squatting on the mean wooden bench against one wall, cuddling the tiny body of Sinatra to her chest, and sobbing as if her world had come to an end.

'Whatever's the matter?' he asked in soft tones. 'Or it your grandfather?' At the sound of his voice, she looked up at him with drowned eyes, and said, 'It's just everything. I can't cope any more.'

Entering the room proper, Garden crouched down beside her, put an arm round her shoulder, and made to offer words of comfort, but not before Sinatra had made a successful attempt to nip him on the wrist. Ignoring this spiteful gesture, he patted Pippa on the back and said, 'Come on, you can tell me. Once you pour it all out, things won't seem half so bad, and I may be able to help in some way.'

'I'm doing everything I can to make changes to this place and make it more of a success, but there are people staying here who were enemies of Granddad, and now they're out to get *me*,' she declared, somewhat melodramatically. 'I have enemies in the hotel.'

'Surely not. Who do you think means you any harm?'

'There are a couple of guests who said that my family acquired certain portions of the hotel in a somewhat underhand manner, and that they're going to law to sort the matter out. They say I can expect to lose parts of the business, and have it back in little bits that are unconnected.'

'Really? How far does this go back?' Garden asked,

although he already knew the answer.'

'Generations,' she nearly spat. 'How am I expected to cope with consequences of things that probably happened before Granddad was born? And there's something else.'

'What?'

'There's a bloke staying here who says that Granddad seduced his wife when they stayed here ages ago, and that they carried on an affair together which resulted in the end of his marriage. He really had it in for Granddad, and I'm scared that it's him who murdered him.' At this, tears began to trickle down her cheeks, and she gave a mighty sniff which seemed to express the unfairness of all this, on top of her responsibility for the whole business now.

'I was supposed to go to college to study hospitality and, although I wasn't very keen on the idea, and wanted to get more into the everyday running of things, being catapulted into total responsibility is very hard to cope with.'

'I'm sure it is. Have you thought of hiring a temporary manager just until you get the hang of things?' asked Garden hoping that this idea may be of some comfort and support to her.

'No way, José!' she snorted. 'If I've got to run the whole shebang, then I do it on my own.' The vehemence of her answer made him move away from her in alarm.

'Have you sought any legal advice?' asked her would-be comforter. 'Do you know who your grandfather's solicitor was?'

'I never had reason to ask him, but I'm sure there must be some record of who dealt with all his legal work in the office.' She was a little calmer now.

'You go and look it out and give whoever it is a ring: tell them about the trouble you're having. Then get on to the people who are threatening you with legal action, and get their solicitors to contact yours, and let them work on it together. There's nothing you can do on your own – I mean, you don't have a law degree, so it's not worth wasting stress on until the experts have had a chew on the actual evidence, is there?'

'No,' she replied with a watery smile. 'You're right. I'll go and look through his papers right away.'

'The details should be somewhere with his will, if nowhere else,' suggested Garden helpfully, 'And, as for the guy whose marriage has broken up, I suggest you give his details to the police, so that they can investigate whether he was the one who killed your grandfather. They may know nothing about that rather personal beef with him.'

'You've been very kind,' she said, kissing Sinatra on the head and rising to her feet. 'Thank you for your time and concern Mr, er …'

'Garden. John Garden.'

'John Garden, you are a very kind man,' she stated without a trace of embarrassment, and leaned forward and hugged him, much to his discomfiture. Before he left, however, he did have the foresight to ask one more question. 'Could you let me have the names of the three people who have been causing you distress, and I'll see if there's anything I can do.'

'Of course. Mr Staywell is the one whose marriage broke up, Mr Carrington and Ms Harrison are the ones who want to dispute ownership. And just to put the tin lid on things, first thing this morning, I got a call from a local estate agent saying that one of his clients is staying here and would like to purchase the property. I feel like all the hounds of hell are after me at the moment.'

'I'm sure you do. You certainly have a lot on your plate, but leave it to me and my partner.' Here, Garden's chest actually swelled a little with self-importance. 'He and I have a private investigation bureau, and I can assure you that, as of now, we are on the case for you.'

'Wow! Private detectives? How unusual. I can't pay

you much, though.'

'I wasn't looking for payment. Take it as a complimentary opening offer from our bureau.'

'Fine words butter no parsnips' never even entered his mind. 'And the name of the person who wishes to purchase the hotel? This is just for investigative purposes, you understand?'

'Josephine Hughes. But she can't force me to sell to her if I don't want to. If the others get their way, though, and get their hands on part of the hotel, then I suppose there would be nothing else I could do. I couldn't afford to pay the other two off, whereas she might have enough to do just that.'

Holmes was hopelessly enchanted by the tale that Garden told of the encounter he had had with the hotel's young owner on his daily search for his room, and beamed at Garden as if he had just won the lottery. 'You know what that means, don't you?' he asked, somewhat enigmatically.

'No idea, Holmes, but I'm sure you're going to tell me.'

'It means we have a whole new nest of suspects to look at, and with a fine variety of reasons for them to have turned murderer.'

'Do we?'

'But of course. Property disputes, like neighbourly disputes, bring out the worst in people, and Berkeley Bellamy was the first likely victim with such things. If two people say he doesn't own all of this property, which we already knew but didn't realise the significance of, it could be either one of them. Similarly, if someone wants to get hold of this as a business opportunity, the first move would be to destabilise the management somehow, and how better than to murder the owner? Then there's our cuckolded husband. Now, there's a motive for murder, if ever I saw one.'

'But how do the other two deaths fit in, though?'

'All in good time. If we can sort out who committed the initial murder, it may answer the question of why the other two had to go as well.'

'If you say so,' muttered Garden, with little conviction. 'I'll believe you, but thousands wouldn't. But just before you go off on a tangent, what about all those suspects we painstakingly interviewed yesterday?'

'What about them?'

'Do you think they're all innocent?'

'Absolutely not, old boy, but we need a complete picture of events before we draw any definite conclusions.'

This sounded, to Garden, the fudge that it actually was, and he went on more forcefully, 'Do you not fancy any of those women? Come on, tell me. In the order that we visited them, we'll start with Miss Fitch.'

'Guilty,' replied Holmes.

'Motive?' asked Garden.

'Jealousy,' replied Holmes.

'OK, Miss Merrilees?

'Guilty.'

'Motive?'

'Jealousy.'

'Miss Crumpet?'

'Guilty as charged.'

'Motive?'

'Revenge.'

Revenge? At least it was a different answer.

'Or, perhaps jealousy,' replied Holmes, this time hedging his bets.

Garden sighed. 'Mabs and Lebs?' He couldn't wait to hear what Holmes had to say about this couple.

'Guilty.'

'Why?'

'Mabs, to get access to Pippa. Lebs, because she's really bisexual and not lesbian, and was jealous of all the other women with whom Bellamy had had relationships. But, on the other hand, Mabs might do it out of jealousy, because she knows Lebs is really bisexual and wants to remove the competition,'

Garden threw his hands in the air and declared that he gave up. 'How can they all be guilty?'

'Well, they just might be. I haven't made up my mind yet who has the strongest motive.'

'I'll tell you now, if anything happens to you, it'll be me that's responsible, because I could throttle you, the way you're sitting on the fence. I thought you were going to be the great detective?'

'I am. That's why I'm being so cautious. I don't want to say something rash and then be proved a fool. Can we get on with our new suspects now?'

His expression was so like that of an eager puppy that Garden agreed just so as not to upset his new friend, but great detective he was not proving to be, which he confirmed unequivocally by looking Garden straight in the eye and saying, 'If I think they're all guilty, at least I'll be right on one of them. Unless, of course, it's a conspiracy, and they're all in it together.'

'Oh, grow up. Who do you think you are, Agatha Christie? I see no trains,' replied Garden, waspishly, in a reference to one of the queen's more famous books.

Chapter Thirteen

Still Tuesday

The news swept round the hotel like wildfire. Chef had been arrested and taken into the police station for questioning. The place was buzzing with speculation. It had been no secret that the cook and the previous owner disagreed about the contents of the menu, and those who lived locally were all on Chef's side. A bit of variety would make them return more often to eat there, and it was only fair that the man be given a chance to prove his worth. His attitude was injurious to business, and had definitely held the place back.

The thought that Chef could have actually done away with him just to cook more interesting and up-to-date food though, seemed ludicrous. Then there was the general memory of how short Chef's fuse was, and how quick his temper to rise to storm force. Maybe he *had* found it in himself to commit such an act.

When they heard what had happened, Holmes and Garden went straight to the bar to cross-question William Byrd and seek his opinion of the likelihood of the head of catering being a murderer.

'He had a rare old temper on him when roused,' Byrd told them. 'I have known him lump one of the sous chefs just for cutting the onions across instead of down, and dicing the cucumber instead of slicing it. Everything had to be done his way – I suppose because he had no control of the dishes that his kitchen served, he exerted his power over how things were prepared and served.

'And I did hear Bellamy and he having a scrap when we first got here,' added Garden, suddenly remembering what he had heard on one of his, now familiar, wanders.

'But I would have expected a chef to use one of his kitchen knives,' said Holmes, a little predictably.

'Why? Shoving him out of a window was a lot more anonymous. If the police had found his body attacked with a kitchen knife, they would have taken Chef away within half an hour of the murder. It was his idea of being subtle, maybe.'

'Did anyone hear him issue any threats to the previous owner?' asked Garden, becoming pragmatic.

'After an argument, he was always thinking up ways to get his own back on the man, but it was all hot air. He used to make some of the waitresses' hair stand on end, though. He could sound very bloodthirsty.'

'And was he believed?' Garden again.

'No! Everyone knew it was just bluster and injured pride, along with his professional frustration at being so controlled.'

'So, you don't think he did it?' asked Holmes, suddenly joining in the conversation again.

'Now, I didn't say that, did I?' squirmed Byrd. 'I just said he was usually all hot air.'

Giving up on nailing the man down to anything like an opinion, Holmes ordered a pot of coffee to be served to them in the guests' lounge, and set off at a brisk pace to this objective, with Garden in his wake, waving apologetically to the barman, and wondering whom his new partner would turn to next as main suspect.

He was beginning to get the feeling that, if they gelled as a partnership, he was the one who would be doing the bulk of the detecting, while Holmes just blustered and took care of the bills. Not that he minded. He'd just like to know where he stood.

In the guests' lounge, settled on matching chesterfield sofas, Garden poured their refreshment while Holmes scanned the other residents scattered around the large room. With a sigh of triumph, he carefully pointed at two figures at the bookcase which was situated against the opposite wall. 'See those two?' he asked, in a very carrying and sibilant whisper.

'Shh!' Garden ordered. 'And don't point in such an obvious way. There's no reason to give away the identity of the people you're about to talk about. Anyway, what about them?'

'When I stayed down the other night, they're the ones I joined, in conversation with another man. They're the two who are in dispute about ownership of parts of this hotel. The other man, I believe, was a solicitor. We need to speak to them.'

'Don't you think we need to approach the solicitor first, just so that we don't make monumental fools of ourselves? He won't talk to us, you know.'

'He might,' said Holmes with a superior smirk, 'if we present him with our official business cards. He'll no doubt see us as allies on the road to justice for his clients.'

Garden was not so sure of this, but didn't dare suggest going straight to the other hotel guests and accusing them of murder. 'Do you reckon it's a local solicitor then, that they're using?'

'I believe so,' replied Holmes, with his fingers crossed out of sight, for luck. 'And what was the name of that woman who wants to buy the place?'

'Ms Hughes. I suggest we go and consult with Mr Budge, whom we saw when we viewed the office premises. If she hasn't already been to see him, then I'm sure he'll have his snout in the local gossip trough, and know who *is* dealing with her. He seemed that sort of person to me.'

'Well said, Garden. And we can have a bit of a puff on

the way, without any dirty looks. No one can complain about us having a smoke out in the open air. This is still a free country.'

'And I'd better have another little batch of our cards printed. We do seem to be giving them out at a rather fast rate.'

Justin Budge was in his office and available to see them when they turned up just after lunch for a little chat. Business was definitely not booming, as evidenced not just by his lack of appointments, but by the lack of sold signs on the few properties he had on display in his windows. Maybe the very slight recovery in the property market had stalled.

He greeted them heartily, however, and bade them take a seat as he used the internal phone to order coffee for three. 'How can I help you?' he asked, a big, cheesy grin on his face, rather like that of the wolf when it saw Grandma was too weak and ill to run away from his ravening jaws.

Holmes reached into his inside jacket pocket and took out one of the little cards that were hot off the press, and handed it over without a word.

'Ah, I see. So that's why you were after office premises. Is this a new venture, or an expansion of an existing successful business?'

Cheeky-looking ornament, thought Holmes, as he tapped the side of his nose with a knowing wink, in the hope of giving a very dishonest impression. Garden had to hold on to the muscles of his jaw so that it didn't drop open with surprise. What was the old man playing at?

But Justin Budge was just the sort of person to fall for Holmes' feint to the left, and he winked back conspiratorially. 'Got you, Mr Holmes. How can I be of assistance?'

What? Was it going to be so easy with this character?

Yes. 'We're currently making enquiries about a lady called Josephine Hughes,' declared Holmes with great confidence, having dredged the lady's name out of one of the obscure recesses of his memory, even though he had only recently filed it.

'Ah, the charming Josephine. She's not all she seems, is she?' Budge asked, with another knowing wink. 'I had an appointment with her just after you first viewed your new offices' – he emphasised these last three words, infusing them with a degree of personal pride – 'and she'd told me at a previous meeting that she was looking for a property in the area.

'I, of course, had looked out several substantial residential properties for her perusal, but it turned out that what she wanted to get her hands on was The Black Swan. A very successful businesswoman, is our Josephine, and she could certainly afford to buy it. The only fly in the ointment had been Bellamy's absolute refusal to budge on the fact that he would never let the hotel go out of his family, and they were at stalemate.'

'So, what was she expecting you to be able to do for her?' asked Garden astutely.

'She thought if I went round and opened a casual conversation about values in the area and how they'd risen, and how his place would be worth a fortune, he could sell up his old pile, buy Pippa something smaller to work on while she was learning her trade, and still walk away with shedloads of money.

'Thing was, she'd made her first approach to me a couple of days before I met you guys and, although I said I'd talk to him the very next day, by the time I got around to seriously considering going up there, he was already dead. The day you looked over your office premises, we were going to discuss where to go next.

'I reckoned the whole lot would go to his granddaughter, and that she'd be greedy to become a rich woman at her age, set up for the rest of her life.'

'And have you talked to her yet?' asked Holmes, now very interested.

'I was going to visit her yesterday, but I got a call from Josephine to say that she'd had a word herself, and the little cat had screamed in her face that she was a vulture who couldn't wait to pick the dead flesh from her grandfather's corpse, and that she'd see her in hell before she even considered selling to her.'

'So you never did get up there to speak to either of them?'

'No. I'm afraid I didn't.' Budge looked glum at this lack of success. A sale of this magnitude would have meant a considerable profit for him personally, and he mourned its loss as if it had been a flesh and blood friend.

'I don't suppose you could give us an idea of just how much the place is worth, could you?' asked Garden.

Budge mouthed an impossibly high figure at them across the table, and his two visitors both whistled at the same time, at the magnitude of the sum involved. 'I don't suppose either of you gentlemen would be interested, if I could persuade the fair Pippa?'

'Sorry, old chap,' Holmes consoled him, 'but that's completely out of our league.' Although he could have personally afforded it with his unexpected windfall, he wasn't going to let anyone know that, not even Garden. He would be setting himself up as an Aunt Sally once word got around, and it would, almost by a process of osmosis. No, he wanted to keep that information so close to his chest, it would appear to be tattooed on to the skin.

Back in the hotel garden, where a weak sun was driving away the last of the persistent mist that had looked like it would remain for the rest of the day, Garden asked what their next step should be, although he now realised he could not rely on Holmes to anywhere near live up to his namesake.

146

'We've got to visit the solicitor before we tackle any of the guests, but I believe a spot of refreshment is on the cards right now, just to bolster up our blood sugar before we tangle with a member of the legal profession. Eels are easier to handle than solicitors.'

Martin Pryke, on being contacted by telephone, said he could fit in an interview with them just before he closed for the day, but was rather sniffy when Holmes would not disclose to him the nature of their business, and evidently was dismissing them as time-wasters.

This was confirmed by his offhand attitude when he invited them into his office, evidently judging that it would not be long before they left it again. 'How can I be of assistance to you gentlemen?' he asked, with a tiny curl of his upper lip, giving just the ghost of a sneer.

Holmes handed over one of their now-indispensable business cards and waited for the man's response. Pryke gave it a glance, then put his chin on to the bridge of his intertwined fingers and just stared at them. Garden stared back, but Holmes fell for the silent treatment and began to bluster.

Pryke's face was growing a smile, and Garden butted in at this inauspicious sign, to save his partner embarrassment. 'We're here about the cases of unlawful acquisition of parts of The Black Swan hotel carried out in the past by the Bellamy family. We know there are two different cases involving two completely uninvolved parties. We would like to know exactly which parts of the hotel are in dispute, and what you think are the chances of a successful outcome for your clients.' He was concise and to the point, and Holmes regarded him warmly with approval.

'I am not at liberty to discuss my clients' business with total strangers,' replied Pryke, with a smug little grin.

'Maybe not, but I assume these cases will wend their

way to court, where the information will then be in the public domain. We only want to know which parts of the building are disputed, not the ins and outs of the legalities of the situations.'

'No can do, old chap, what with professional confidentiality.' Pryke was enjoying himself enormously at their expense, and using one of their own weapons against them.

'But we're fellow professionals,' blustered Holmes, now going purple in the face with indignation.

'I think not. I had to study for years to get my present qualifications. How long and what did you study to get to the point where you can hand out spurious business cards?'

'I've never been so insulted in all my life,' barked Holmes, rising to his feet.

'You should get out more, then,' replied Pryke, and gave an oily little giggle.

'Come along, Garden. We don't need to stay here to be insulted.'

'No? Where do you usually go?'

'Insufferable little man!' were Holmes' final words, as he stamped out of the offices and back outside. 'How dare he?'

'He's right, though,' replied Garden, unhelpfully.

'That's not the point. We'll find out what we need to know straight from the horses' mouths.'

'What do you mean?'

'You wait and see. I have a cunning plan.'

'Do you?'

'Well, almost.'

Garden sighed deeply. Holmes may be a great name for a detective, but this one didn't seem to have an investigative bone in his body. It looked like he lived the life of an easily distracted butterfly who couldn't put two and two together nor make a decision about which suspect was the most likely to be guilty.

It looked like, in their future together, Holmes would have the name that would attract the clients and he, Garden, would be the brains of the outfit. It was all the wrong way round but, then, as Holmes had previously pointed out to him, fiction if fiction. This was real life, and not a mirror.

Both fledgling detectives were in the bar early that evening, in the guise of stalking horses. They knew that most residents popped in for a drink before dinner, and that the two guests involved in the legal disputes were likely to eat together to discuss tactics.

'I did sit with these people the other night, you know,' declared Holmes, yet again. 'And I did gather a bit about what was going on but, at the time, I was too taken up with the members of the Ladies' Guild to think about them seriously as suspects. A portion of a hotel does beat jealousy, hands down though, don't you think?'

'Not to mention the desire to actually acquire the ownership of the place. Let's hope we really get lucky tonight, and manage to engage the right people in conversation.' Garden was not the optimist that Holmes was, and thought it just as likely that none of those they wished to question would show their faces.

But he was wrong, and the first new suspect to approach the bar was Josephine Hughes, clearly on her own. This was a signal for Holmes to go back to the bar, offer to buy her drink, and ask her if she would like to join them for a little pre-prandial conversation.

Completely unsuspecting, and noting the respectability with which the man who had issued the invitation was dressed, she accepted with alacrity, and immediately joined Garden at the table, Holmes on her heels with two glasses in his hands. She did give Garden a slightly strange glance, but he was, for him, dressed fairly conservatively in lemon shirt, lime tie, and bottle-green trousers, and his tidiness and cleanliness – if not his godliness – could not be doubted.

'Allow me to introduce you to my new business partner, Mr Garden,' said Holmes. 'We are currently setting up a new branch of our business in this town, and will be here for a few more days.'

'How exciting for you,' replied Josephine. As if the subject closest to her heart had been triggered, which it had, she immediately began to talk about her own reasons for being here.

'I'm a businesswoman of some standing, and I'd heard about this place long before I came here. Some business colleagues of mine have stayed here and remarked on its unique character, so I came down for myself to assess it, and immediately fell in love. I'd dearly love to acquire it for my business portfolio, but no luck so far.'

'Never give up,' Holmes said in encouragement.

'Oh, I don't intend to. I can be very determined when I want something, and I want this hotel so badly now, it's beginning to hurt. Think how I could market something like this to parties of touring Americans. They'd just lap it up. All those ancient beams and rambling corridors would have them delirious with delight.'

At that moment, Niles Carrington and Jane Harrison entered the bar, engrossed in conversation, and Holmes excused himself to approach them and remind them that he had had a drink with them recently, ending up inviting them to join his table. He knew that those who have a grievance, and an inevitable gospel to preach on the subject, love spreading the word and pulling in support from others.

Soon there were five of them round a middle-sized table, and Garden was cleverly drawing the two newcomers out, about why they were staying there. That inevitably brought Josephine Hughes into the conversation, as she saw an opportunity here. If she could oversee the splitting up of the ownership, it would be easier to pick up two part-owners than one owner of the complete business, and maybe buy them off – she could certainly afford it and, what, after all, would they do with a tiny bit of the whole venture? The very idea defied the imagination.

Holmes was discreetly efficient at keeping the drinks coming, to loosen tongues, and it worked. Within just over half an hour, their stories were on the table for scrutiny, all three of the other guests supporting each other's bid for justice and ownership.

At this point, Garden slipped away, saying he had some business to attend to, and returned, much to Holmes' consternation, twenty minutes later, as his female persona of the night before. Greeting his astonished partner with a husky, 'Good evening, Sherman. Haven't you got a drink waiting for me? You know how I like a white-wine spritzer.'

Holmes rose like a marionette, the strings of which had all just been jerked taut, and tottered towards the bar, at a total loss as to what Garden was up to, pulling a stunt like this without warning.

Garden knew what he was doing, however, and said he'd noticed them all in the bar when he was in there the previous evening. As two of them had noticed him sitting across the room, it was an automatic in, especially when he said he'd been done wrong by the previous owner, and the knives really came out.

Josephine Hughes was first to bare her personal grudge. 'He called me a money-grubbing swindler who would stoop to any depths to get my own way, and that what I needed was servicing by a decent man, then offered himself up to do the job.'

'How incredibly insulting,' commiserated Garden.

'He accused my family of being so twisted and crooked

151

that we resembled corkscrews, and said my forefathers would cheat a widow out of her last farthing. I'll have you know that my great-grandfather died in the workhouse, having lost everything he had in his transaction with the Bellamy family with the workshop he used to have on a small piece of land out at the back of the hotel.' This was Jane Harrison's tale of woe, quickly followed by Niles Carrington's, as he would not be outdone by two women.

'My great-grandfather and his father owned a small business on the eastern corner of the hotel, and they thought they were renting it out to the hotel, but neither of them could read or write, and it was one of the Bellamys that misread the document of transfer to them.

'He persuaded them it was for rental only, and to put their mark with confidence, when the document was actually for the sale of the premises, and they lost their livelihood, and my great-grandfather threw himself in the river at the disgrace that his lack of education had brought on him and his family. What about you, Ms ... I'm afraid we don't know your name.'

'Miss Watts,' replied Garden, not going the whole hog. 'Joanne. It was nothing really disastrous for me: just a little business deal that looked like I was going to be the loser. When it seemed to be on track, he was all over me. When I realised he was trying to swindle me, it was a different story, and I'm afraid he was very insulting about my personal attractions.'

At this, he sniffed, extracted a minuscule lace handkerchief from his tiny evening bag, and held it delicately to the corner of each eye, as if absorbing tears. 'Don't upset yourself, Joanne,' purred Niles Carrington, putting his hand on Garden's knee.

'Thank you so much for listening to me, but I'm afraid I must be off.' That hand on the knee had certainly made Garden jump. He hadn't expected to be found attractive, and have someone make a move on him. 'I only called in tonight to see that Sherman was alright. Ah, there you are, Sherman, dearest,' he called out, seeing the familiar face entering the bar, once more. 'I'm off now, but I'll give you a ring in a few days to see how things are going.'

'Lovely to see you again so soon,' improvised Holmes, to receive a radiant smile from Garden, that the older man had not given away his identity in his initial surprise and confusion. 'Goodbye.'

'TTFN, Sherman,' Garden's husky voice rasped out, and he sashayed out of the bar, and out of the other three people's lives, for ever. But, if nothing else, the presence of his alter ego seemed to have got the conversation on a more flowing footing, especially as he claimed to have had a bad experience with Berkeley Bellamy. So much for their solicitor's discretion and professional confidentiality! They probably wouldn't have minded if Holmes had got out their individual case files and gone through every sheet of paper in them.

Chapter Fourteen

Wednesday

An unusually brave choice of bacon, eggs, pancakes, and maple syrup was efficiently being demolished – Holmes having gone uncharacteristically American in his choice of breakfast – as Garden questioned his partner on what he'd thought of the three people they'd talked to the night before, but Holmes would not be distracted from his main beef.

'Don't you ever do that to me again, young Garden. I nearly had a heart attack when you came back to the bar in your girl's gear.'

'But that's exactly how I should use it. Those three were sitting with a couple of regular guys, and suddenly a sympathetic woman joined you when your insignificant other – i.e. me – had to go to attend to something else. Once I said that Bellamy hadn't treated me very well, they were off and unloading. Joanne Watts draws people out. She's our secret weapon, as we said before. Where people might not talk to a man, they'll happily spill everything to a woman.'

Holmes speared a morsel of bacon with his fork, dipped it in the yolk of his egg, and added a piece of syrupy pancake to the mouthful. For about twenty seconds he sat thoughtfully chewing, then said, 'Do you know, I think you're right. And I assume that Joanne Watts is the name you gave them for your alter ego.'

'It is, but it's a moveable feast. I have several wigs in

different styles and colours, and I can really be whoever I like. I could make you look like a right lothario.'

'Steady on, old man. Can't have that. But what you say is very interesting. It means that "Holmes and Garden" actually has at least three detectives, one or more of them which could be women if we wanted them to.'

'Exactly.' Garden sat in silence after this, allowing the situation to gel in Holmes' mind. 'I think it could be our undercover USP,' he added.

'Dear boy, I do believe you're right. Now, what were you asking me about last night?'

'What did you think of the three people we got to spill their personal beans? Let's start with Josephine Hughes.'

'Guilty,' declared Holmes. Garden sighed. This was sounding familiar, but he'd have to see the thing through.

'Motive?'

'Commercial greed.'

'Niles Carrington?'

'Guilty.'

'Jane Harrison?'

'Guilty.'

'But you can't just say guilty to everyone.' Garden was getting frustrated with his friend. He seemed incapable of making decisions in eliminating anyone who had been on their hitherto unwritten list of suspects. What was wrong with the man?

'What motives?'

'Business ruthlessness, revenge, and revenge, in that order.'

'Holmes, we're supposed to be solving these murders, not just accusing all and sundry of committing them.'

'We'll get there. I just need to cogitate a while.'

'And how do you intend to do that?'

'We're off to an auction of office furniture about twenty miles away today – viewing this morning and sale this afternoon. That'll give my subconscious plenty of time to play with what we know, and come up with a single culprit.'

There the man went again, skipping off gaily down a tangent without a thought of what they probably ought to be doing. 'You're not investigating today?'

'*We're* not investigating today. By the way, when I was coming along the corridor, I heard the dulcet tones of Chef bawling out one of his sous chefs, so he must have been released from police custody.'

'Hang on a minute. Let me get this straight. I'm going with you to this auction?'

'Got to choose your own desk, my boy. Got to choose your own desk.'

Garden was simply dumbfounded by Holmes' laid-back attitude, and couldn't understand why he was taking their first case so lightly, and flounced off to his room to change into something more colourful, if they were going out.

Joining Holmes outside where he was having a puff on his pipe, the older man looked up, dropped his head, then looked up again in a double-take of surprise. 'Are you auditioning for something on children's television?' he asked, letting his gaze run up and down Garden's colourful form.

'No, I just wanted to wear something that made me feel happy,' replied the younger man, not adding that Holmes' attitude to detection had so depressed him that he needed something to lift his spirits. He had on royal blue trousers, a turquoise shirt, and a green tie, bottomed off with blood red lace-up shoes. 'I'll walk ten paces behind you, if you like,' he added, grumpily.

'Don't be silly. You're a very cheering sight. You just took me by surprise, that's all.'

'Well, at least you won't have to cope with Joanne today.'

'That would have thrown me, but I've taken on board what you said, and I truly believe she could be a real, er, asset to our business.' Garden fought the thought that if Holmes didn't buck up his ideas, there wouldn't be a business.

'Come on,' urged Holmes, 'Let's go and "desk-up", and we'll have some lunch at a country pub after the viewing.'

The auction was to be held in an old church, many years past its use as a place of worship, the congregation having evaporated over time like a puddle on a hot day. There was an eclectic collection of "office" furniture on view, and the two men walked around peering at each item to evaluate its usefulness to them in their new offices.

Holmes had posted his resignation from work on the way, but Garden still had his in his room. He was getting unnerved about taking the final step by Holmes' peculiar attitude of thinking every suspect guilty, and even considered that he might be able to mend a bridge sufficiently to be able to move back in with his mother, such was his consternation.

It was Holmes who had bought a catalogue, and was busy marking items in it for bidding on in the afternoon. Garden was more fascinated with the lots that seemed to have nothing to do with office life, such as a hugely fringed standard lamp, and an over-sized walnut wardrobe. Whoever would have those in their place of work? How had they managed to insinuate themselves into a sale of office furniture?

'See any desks you fancy?' asked Holmes, suddenly stopping in mid-stride.

'Don't really mind, so long as there's room for a laptop and a set of filing trays,' replied Garden, 'and I can get my legs under it.'

'What about a chair?'

'One that doesn't wobble or suddenly collapse downwards would be fine. I mean, I'm only going to sit on it, and I rather hoped that most of our time would be spent out on cases.'

'Of course, of course,' replied Holmes, whose mind this thought had not had the decency to cross. At the moment he couldn't see further than sitting at a rather grand oak affair in a captain's chair, and looking important.

'And don't forget filing cabinets,' Garden prompted him.

'I thought we might go for what I've heard referred go as a paperless office,' was Holmes' response.

'No such thing. What about evidence? What about correspondence? What about reports and invoicing? What about contracts with clients?'

'Bum!'

'That's not very helpful,' commented Garden.

'No, but it made me feel better. Do you want to see what I've marked?'

'Do I have to?'

'Where's your enthusiasm? This is a new life we're furnishing this afternoon.'

'I suppose so.'

Garden barely concentrated as Holmes excitedly pointed to lumps of wood, lumps of wood and leather, and even glass and steel, but was revived by a superb lunch in a pub only a few hundred yards away from the old building. Although he had eaten a good breakfast, it had not dispelled any of his fears about his partner. Lunch, for some reason, made him feel more confident.

Maybe it was just the thought that the office would soon be a reality, and he could always put off resigning for a while by taking all of his remaining annual leave in a block. That way he could hedge his bets and see how the business progressed, once it had opened properly.

Perhaps it was just the thought that if Holmes and Garden didn't get off to a flying start, his new partner was sufficiently wealthy to carry the business until such times as it started to show a profit. If it ever did. And did it matter, so long as Holmes was willing to carry on? Probably not, and he could jump ship anytime if an opportunity of a more conventional position reared its head.

Back in the old church once more, Garden couldn't help noticing that, no matter how long an ecclesiastical establishment had not been used as such, it always retained its unique smell. He let his thoughts wander, as Holmes began to flick his catalogue in bidding, and he didn't surface again until he heard the auctioneer's gavel go down, and a lugubrious voice intone, 'Sold for five hundred and fifty pounds.' God, someone had paid a lot for something from what he thought was mostly a collection of junk.

At this point, Holmes poked him in the ribs with his catalogue and said, 'I had to go high, but I got it in the end.'

'What? Was that you paying all that money for something? Whatever did you buy?'

'A desk.'

'A solid gold one?'

'No, a rather nice oak kneehole with a leather-tooled top.'

'What was the estimate, for heaven's sake?' asked the younger man, making a grab for the catalogue and searching for the item his partner had just bought. 'Two hundred to two hundred and fifty pounds, it says here. You paid more than twice that.'

'I wanted it.'

'That badly?'

'It's taken me a while to realise, although I don't want you to spread this around, that whatever I want I can have now, and if that means paying twice as much for an attractive desk that I shall get a lot of pleasure from sitting behind, then so be it. I didn't want any new furniture. It smacks of new business, and I want us to look long-established.'

'Mad as a hatter.' Garden was dumbfounded, then wondered if he'd have done the same in Holmes' position. Probably, he would. The cavalier attitude to price with which Holmes purchased a further attractive desk and two swivelling captain's chairs raised his spirits considerably, as he realised that there needed to be no financial success whatsoever to their business venture. Holmes was playing, and that might give him, Garden, the opportunity to develop into a real detective. What a God-given chance for him to train on the job, while being paid at the same time.

The next forty minutes saw the purchase of a secretary's desk and chair, and a selection of old filing cabinets made from a beautifully aged oak. They were definitely class, and looked as if they actually dated from Conan Doyle's lifetime. How things could change, once a situation was fully and properly evaluated. He'd post his letter of resignation as soon as he got back to the hotel.

His attitude to his new friend, rather cold this morning, warmed considerably, as he contemplated a very enjoyable future. He didn't mind at all being the brainy one.

At the end of the sale some miscellaneous items came under the hammer, and Holmes remained to bid for, and win, some beautiful old Persian rugs that were far too big for most people's living rooms, given today's housing, and would not have appealed to a younger set.

The auction had finished by four o'clock, and Holmes left the building rubbing his hands together with glee. 'Well, that's that sorted, then,' said Garden, by way of opening a conversation.

'Not quite, John H. We've got another port of call before we're finished for the day.'

'Where?'

'A computer superstore, so that we can get what we need to usher us into the twenty-first century. Only the best for our business. Oh, and I don't suppose you brought your laptop with you when you booked into the hotel, did you?'

'Absolutely not, but we could go home via my old home, and you could use it there. Or we could swing by your place.'

'It wouldn't do any good. I don't own such a thing. No, we'll call round and see if your delightful mother is at home. Maybe she can offer us a cup of tea.

'No!'

'Yes! You must start facing up to your fears, which I know you realise were basically unfounded or, if they were founded, were founded in guilt and hysteria.'

'I suppose so.' John H. was slightly hurt by this comment, and had no desire whatsoever to see his mother again so soon after their last visit. She'd acted in such a normal way that he thought she must have been possessed by a mischievous spirit, and not been herself at all.

After what seemed like huge expenditure in a high-tech store, Holmes drove to Garden's old address, and they were lucky enough to find Mrs Garden just home from her temping job.

'Hello, Johnny, darling. How lovely to see you,' she said, and kissed her son on the cheek. He put his hand to this face as if he'd just been stung, and pulled his features into a grimace of distaste, but she didn't notice. 'And Mr Holmes, how lovely to see you again so soon. Shall I put on the kettle?'

'That would be divine, dearest lady,' replied Holmes, his cheeks flushing just a slight shade of pink.

Garden fetched his laptop from his locked and padlocked bedroom and put it on the dining table for

Holmes' use. He hadn't wanted to take it to the hotel, for there was always a chance of someone either stealing it, or taking a look at his private files. His make-up tips were top secret, and he wouldn't share them with anyone, not even his mother. Especially not his mother.

'If you haven't got a laptop, do you actually know how to use a computer?' asked Garden, who had been pondering this point since Holmes admitted that he didn't own such a machine.

'Of course I do. I just couldn't see a place for it in my apartment. I had as much access as I wanted to the cyber world at work, but as I've now resigned, I need to get myself kitted out.' Holmes removed a tiny notebook from an inner pocket and consulted some notes he had made, which proved to be websites of the sort that sold security equipment and listening devices – tiny cameras, bugs, and suchlike.

'Are you really doing what I think you're doing?' asked Garden, scandalised.

'Of course I am. We can't trade without surveillance equipment. Even you should know that. I know Holmes managed with just the Baker Street Irregulars, but times have changed, and these little beauties will be our eyes and ears on the job.'

'I never thought of that.'

'Well, how many ragamuffin children do you know who would do our spying for us for just a ha'penny or a farthing?'

'I get your point.'

'You're going to have to stop being such an upright citizen, Garden, or we'll get nowhere.'

Holmes could surprise John H. at every turn. Maybe he wasn't as useless as he had thought earlier. Only time would tell.

When they returned to The Black Swan, Holmes suggested

that they go up to his room for a snifter, to take stock of just what they had purchased today, and to consider whether they needed anything else before they started publicly trading. As they passed the little library room in which the Ladies' Guild had held their committee meetings, they both noticed a sign on the door. As well as a 'do not disturb' sign on the door, there was another one in block capitals. 'PLEASE DO NOT ENTER. PRIVATE MEETING IN PROGRESS.'

'I wonder what all that's about?' queried Garden.

'No idea, but I'll ask Byrd when we get downstairs. He'll know, because there'll probably be an order for liquid refreshments at some point during the evening.'

It took only one nip of malt for them to realise that all they were really missing was stationery, signage, and advertising. Printers, telephones, and answering machines they had picked up at the high-tech store, as well as their top-of-the-range computers and slightly less-expensive laptop for what Holmes regarded as an actuality – their secretary in the outer office. Garden had argued with him that such a person did not exist but so insistent was Holmes that she would in the very near future that he had given up the unequal battle.

Both men were quite tired after their day of high expenditure, so they just had a bar meal that evening and both retired early. On his way into his room, Holmes noticed that the private meeting still seemed to be in progress in the small meeting room.

Chapter Fifteen

Thursday

Garden spent rather a disturbed night, as there seemed to be quite a high level of noise both inside and outside the hotel, but he merely put in some earplugs, without which he never stayed anywhere, and achieved a sufficient amount of sleep to satisfy his minimum needs.

The same could not be said of Holmes, however, whom he found sitting in the bar room with a large mug of coffee before him, and eyes that could only be described as p*ss-holes in the snow. His hair was rumpled, and he was incongruously dressed in a pair of old jogging bottoms and a ragged out T-shirt.

'Whatever happened to you?' asked Garden, aghast. 'Have you had an accident?'

'I haven't, but a lot of other people have,' he mumbled enigmatically.

'Has there been a car accident or something?'

'Nothing like that,' Holmes denied, 'but do you remember that private meeting that was taking place last night?'

'Of course I do.'

'Well, they ordered food to be served there, and all of them were carted off just before midnight with what looked and sounded – and smelled,' here, he grimaced at the memory 'very like food poisoning.'

'So why do you look like you've had hardly any sleep at all?'

'Because their cries of pain and distress woke me, and when I went to see what was wrong they were vomiting everywhere – and worse – and I had to call an ambulance and alert someone here. There are hardly any live-in staff, so I was helping get the poor victims out of the room, get them into two ambulances, then helping clean up. It was absolutely disgusting.'

'How foul for you. How many of them were in there?'

'Five,' replied Holmes in a hollow voice, as he remembered the sight that had met his eyes when he had first entered the room.

'And who was having the meeting?' Garden's interest had been piqued now.

'It was the three we spoke to last night, plus the solicitor, and the estate agent, Budge.'

'No! What on earth did they have to eat? I thought Chef was really on his toes now.'

'A share-it seafood platter between all of them.'

'What on earth was in it?'

'Oysters, prawns, scallops, lobster, blue-lipped mussels … You name it, it was on the platter, and enough for each of them to have some of everything.'

'What a ghastly coincidence. My grandmother said never to eat seafood unless there was an R in the month,' Garden informed him.

'And never eat in a hotel where you're in some sort of dispute with ownership.'

'You don't think one of the staff did this on purpose to protect the hotel, do you?'

'I think it's highly probable. So we now have someone else to unmask – someone who wants to protect the place as it is.'

'Have you spoken to anyone?' asked Garden, wondering if they now had two crimes, or just the one, getting bigger and bigger.

'I had a quick chat with Byrd when he came in early for

a delivery, and he said that he'd actually witnessed the booking of the room.'

'I wouldn't have thought Pippa would have let that lot meet on the disputed premises.'

'Apparently it was her who took the booking. Byrd said that she charged them an outrageous price for it, to include food and drinks, then slipped half the money into her back pocket for "a treat for what I have to put up with in this hotel."'

'Anything else?'

'Yes. Uneaten food from the platter as well as samples from the fridge were taken away for analysis, and Chef was arrested as soon as he came in this morning, and has been taken in for questioning again.'

'Good God! And I put in earplugs last night because it seemed so noisy. If only I'd got up to investigate, I could have learnt all this at first hand.'

Holmes winced and gagged. 'You wouldn't have like it. The smell was filthy, as was the mess.'

'I'm going to the kitchen to speak to the other staff. I don't like the sound of this one bit,' declared Garden. Something was nagging at the back of his mind, and only a bit of questioning and letting things churn over together would satisfy him.

'You can't do that till later,' Holmes halted his retreat. 'I arranged for a van to deliver everything from the auction rooms this morning, and the computer firm, as I bunged them an unashamed bribe, said they'd deliver before lunch too. Your excursion to the kitchens will have to wait. It can't be that important.' Garden's guns were spiked before he'd even had time to put balls down the muzzles.

At the offices, the ground floor seemed to be packed to the gunwales with furniture. There was hardly room to swing a Colin, although Garden would have executed such an action with glee, given his current relationship with the

167

animal. 'How did I manage to buy so much?' asked a puzzled Holmes, surveying the sea of oak and other woods.

'I think it's just like the pieces of a jigsaw, Holmes,' said Garden, giving the whole muddle the benefit of his critical eye. 'If we start with one corner, and start to put things where they're going to go, it'll be like the pile of jigsaw pieces – a real muddle, but a tidy flat picture once everything is in the right place.

'Let's put everything that we can into the front office, all piled up together, and then move on to bringing in the pieces that we know go in the back room,' he suggested. Holmes agreed with a nod. He hadn't felt very energetic when Garden had first appeared this morning, after his disturbed night, but the thought of seeing his beloved business as it would be when it was operating gave him the buzz he needed to help lift the heavy pieces of furniture.

Garden was right. Once as much as possible had been removed, it was possible to place the wooden filing cabinets round the walls, and position the desks and their swivel chairs where they thought they would like to be seated. What was left turned out to be just the furniture for the front office, and order was restored within a couple of hours.

There were a few awkward moments when Holmes appeared to be imprisoned behind a huge filing cabinet, in a position that it shouldn't, by the very laws of nature, have been able to get into, but all was finally sorted, and they surveyed their handiwork, abrasions, and minor bruising with pride.

They had only just finished when a van from the hi-tech superstore drew up outside with their order for computers and other electronic supplies and, by the end of the morning, it really looked as if a business had its headquarters in the building.

When the van drove away, Holmes surveyed his

kingdom with pride, rubbed his stomach, and said, 'I'm absolutely starving after that. Coming back for some lunch?'

'Yes,' agreed Garden, similarly empty, 'but not before I've had a little chat in that kitchen.'

On his return, Garden refused to discuss what had happened in the culinary regions in public and, after they had eaten, Holmes was on his feet almost before Garden had the chance to use his napkin. 'Where are you off to?' he asked, puzzled, as he thought they would be talking about what he had learnt earlier.

'Stationer's in the town. They have a sign in their window that promises next-day printing. I want to go in and take a look at what quality of paper and envelopes they offer, and in what fonts they can print. We need some stationery, and we need it fast.'

'Couldn't you order it on the internet? It'd be much cheaper.'

'Cheaper schmeaper!' Holmes exclaimed. 'I told you, I don't need to count the cost of things, and I want to able to touch the paper and feel its quality before I commit myself. Come along. We haven't got all day, you know.'

'Haven't we?'

'No. We're off to see about the design of the signage for the windows after that.'

'You never said anything about all this,' Garden complained.

'That's because I only thought of it while you were away doing whatever it was you felt you had to do in the domestic quarters, so I made a couple of calls and set up appointments for us. No hanging around in a queue for Sherman Holmes, private investigator.' The man puffed out his chest in pride as he uttered these last words. He was really beginning to believe his own myth.

At the stationer's, the woman at the check-out looked at

Holmes in disbelief when he said he had an appointment with the manager but, after she was urged to use the internal phone system, he was proved correct. She watched almost in awe as such a personage as Mr Prendergast came from behind the office door to escort his visitor beyond the reaches of her experience.

Mr Prendergast was not thrown at all by Holmes asking for a personal appointment when his customer informed him of the size his order was likely to be. He also stated that he wanted a large quantity of business cards.

'And what would sir like on the cards? I have a blank here. If you tell me what goes where, we can then get down to discussing the colour of the printing and the font we will use.

Holmes closed his eyes in thought for a moment, and instructed, 'Top right, the address. Across the middle, "Holmes and Garden". Underneath, "Private Investigators". Bottom left, telephone number. Bottom right, "Confidentiality guaranteed".'

'Colour and font?' They were really down to business now.

'White card, black ink, copperplate script,' stated Holmes, with absolute conviction.

'And would sir like a logo?' asked the manager, ever helpful. 'I'll just show you our choice.' And there it was, right at the bottom of the page – a tiny magnifying glass.

'That's the one. That's exactly right. Where would we put it?'

'May I suggest that we put that in the top left-hand corner, which is currently without adornment?'

'Perfect. And will they be ready tomorrow, as advertised by your sign in the window?'

'Of course, sir. Satisfaction guaranteed – rather like your confidentiality, eh?'

Holmes looked at the man blankly, as the little witticism shot right over his head, but Garden made the effort of contributing a little titter of mild amusement.

'Morning or afternoon for collection?'

'Afternoon, I should say, sir, just so that sir is not disappointed.'

'Pleasure doing business with you. Come along, Garden. Things to do, people to see. Good day to you, sir,' he rattled off, and Mr Prendergast found himself looking at a space where they had stood just moments before, and his door swinging closed.

Holmes was just as determined to get what he wanted at the sign-writer's establishment.

'It has to be gold lettering, and I want it in a flowing copperplate.'

'As sir pleases. And what is it you want your signage to say?'

'I want it to say exactly what it does on our business cards, but I won't have one of those to give you until tomorrow. How soon can you do it? I'll pay extra if I don't have to wait.'

'I can do it tomorrow, if sir will pay the premium for quick service.'

'Sir will.'

'Give me the address and a time, and I'll meet you there.'

'You're a gentleman, sir. Any time after lunch.'

'Without fail, sir,' replied the sign-writer, pleased at such a contract in hard times. Many new businesses put up with something painted onto MDF these days. No class, that's what this credit crunch had resulted in – reduced everything to the lowest common denominator – and his business had suffered particularly hard.

Garden pleaded an errand to run before they went through what he had learnt that morning in the kitchen and, although it was exciting news, there was a little job that he had to do first which simply wouldn't wait, so he said he'd meet Holmes in the older man's room when he was finished.

Holmes, who didn't like secrets, harrumphed a bit, but finally gave in with a bad grace and went off to his room, having had to be content with Garden's promise of 'all in good time'.

Nothing can keep an optimist down however, and Holmes positively glowed with pride and excitement as he sat on his bed thinking about how close the offices of his new venture were to actually opening its doors to the public. They'd have to wind things up here, then get Garden moved into his apartment in Farlington Market while they sorted out the decoration and furnishing of the upstairs flat for him.

The thought of seeing Mrs Garden again made him feel all wobbly inside, and he desisted, hoping he wasn't just coming down with something he had caught during his Good Samaritan act of the night before, but pulled himself together when he heard a discreet knock on the door. Garden had arrived.

They sat themselves in the two club chairs that faced the window and Holmes rang room service for a pot of Darjeeling and a plate of crumpets. 'Might as well have afternoon tea, mightn't we? Don't often bother at home, but I do enjoy it when the opportunity arises.' Garden merely nodded, not ever having been in the habit of enjoying anything of the sort. It simply wasn't a meal that was in his family's normal repertoire.

'I learnt some very interesting things in that kitchen earlier,' he began, 'And, on reflection, I think I ought to have told you about it earlier, but you had the first half of the afternoon all planned out, it seemed a pity to spoil your plans.'

'Come on, then, spill the beans, John H.' This sounded promising.

'I spoke to the sous chef, you know, the one with the

terrible acne and the greasy hair.'

'Ugh! I certainly do.'

'I was asking about a seafood platter in general, as if I were going to order one for us, when he ups and says that it's not on the menu. Well, I said I know that something ghastly happened last night with one that was definitely served, and I knew lightning wouldn't strike twice in the same place.

'He told me that he couldn't do one, even for a special order, and that Pippa had taken the order herself, and gone out to get the ingredients for it. She even insisted on preparing it herself as she'd charged so much for it – didn't want to inconvenience any of us, and she'd even take it up herself. She even made the seafood sauce to go over it all.

'When I made a comment about her diligence in seeing that special orders were filled to her satisfaction, one of the washers-up put in that it was no wonder she was giving it her everything. It must be sheer gratitude, because she'd heard that her grandfather was going to change his will if she didn't buckle down to college in September, and pull up her socks with regard to customer satisfaction in the meantime.

'Holy crow!' Holmes gulped. 'That means that it was definitely her that was responsible for the food poisoning. Whether it was a serious attempt on their lives or a warning shot over the bows, we don't yet know, but that room contained what she would regard as all her current enemies, with regard to her ownership of The Black Swan.

'And, if her grandfather was serious about changing his will, maybe she thought she ought to take the chance for full ownership before he changed his mind. She knows all the little nooks and crannies in this place, and could easily have pitched him out of the window before disappearing virtually through a crack in the wall.'

'And maybe the Maitland woman saw her do her

disappearing act, whereas you had your back to her.'

'Ye Gods! I think we're finally getting somewhere, Garden. I told you I was a brilliant detective.'

Garden gave him an old-fashioned look, then his eyes lit up again. 'I've just thought of something else, as well. You remember I heard that maid-cum-waitress having an argument in the linen cupboard with Bellamy. Well, she was pregnant, wasn't she?

'I'd put my shirt on the fact that the baby she was carrying was Bellamy's, and once the rumours got around that she was in the club, it wouldn't be difficult to work out that the baby would be entitled to a slice of this place.

'Well, she couldn't have that happen, could she, so she removed both of her remaining problems, only to have last night's crew materialise as another threat to her kingdom. If La Maitland saw her tossing out her grandfather, then that's the reason she had to be taken care of.

'All those suspects we've had our eye on and wasted time questioning, and the answer was here, right under our noses. We've been as naïve as a couple of work-experience students, not capable of seeing the wood for the trees.'

'Garden, we've solved it!' Holmes was almost dancing with glee and triumph in his chair, and it was all he could do not to get up and do a little jig, but another discreet knock at the door interrupted him, and he called 'come in' without looking round, so excited was he by the prospect of their first successful case. 'Just put it over on the dressing table, will you?' he instructed, while still staring sightlessly out of the window enjoying the unexpected success they had just had in putting the various pieces of the jigsaw together and actually finding out what the picture was.

'You might've solved it, but you're not going to get the chance to share it with anyone, least of all the police. Put your hands where I can see them.'

'What?' The two men whirled round in astonishment at this statement.

'I beg your pardon?'

Both men had turned round to find themselves staring down the barrel of an old World War Two service revolver, and the twisted smile on Pippa's young face.

'What the hell do you think you're going to do?' asked Holmes, at his most indignant.

'Oh, I don't *think* I'm going to do something, I am *definitely* going to do something. I'm going to shoot you two, put the gun into one of your flabby dead hands, then scream the place down. I'll tell them you were a couple of queers who fell out, and one of you killed the other then shot himself.'

Although this sent a chill through Holmes' heart, he had a tiny bit of attention left to notice that Garden seemed fascinated with surreptitiously checking the time on his watch. Holmes glanced down at his own timepiece to see that the second hand was sweeping round to make it almost exactly five o'clock.

He was aware of Garden's whole body tensing as if he were about to start a race, then as the second hand passed the Roman numeral for twelve, the most awful cacophony broke out in the corridor, and Garden sprang like a wild cat at the young woman holding the weapon, kicked it out of her hand, then threw himself onto her body to knock her to the ground. 'Call 999, Holmes, then ring downstairs for staff to help me restrain her.'

Holmes obeyed without a murmur, yelling down the receiver to be heard above the chaotic riot of caterwauling that emanated from just outside the room. When he replaced the receiver, Garden asked him to open the door, whereupon he shouted, that'll do. Thank you. I'll discuss it with you later,' and asked Holmes to shut the door again.

There was total silence for about twenty seconds, then Pippa started yelling, and Holmes asked in a loud voice,

175

'What the hell was that all about?'

Before Garden had time to answer, there was the sound of footsteps clattering up the stairs, and the two sous chefs from the kitchen that Garden had obtained information from earlier entered the room.

The girl did her best, crying out that these two men had attacked her and had intended to rape her, but the two kitchen hands were not stupid, and could put two and two together as well as any other employee of the hotel.

They looked to Garden for instruction and, after informing them that the police were on the way, asked them to help escort the young woman downstairs where they could secure her hands to a chair back, and wait for the forces of law and order to arrive. Before they took her, however, he had something he wanted to clarify with her.

'When I came across you in the boot cupboard, you were sobbing your heart out as if your world were about to come to an end. Were they really just crocodile tears?'

'Of course not,' she spat. 'How on earth could I have had any idea that you might come to the door and hear me? I was devastated by the thought of all that I'd done to secure this place as mine, and now there were three other people queuing up to try to wrest it, or parts of it, from my grasp. I was weeping for the cruelty of Fate that could even consider whipping this opportunity away from me after all I'd been through.'

'And what about the people that you "removed"? Do you not think they may have gone through a horrendous ordeal, too? You killed them, you do realise?'

'Of course I know what I've done, but they were a waste of skin, the whole lot of them. I was the future of this hotel, not some outsider that didn't know their arse from their elbow as far as this place was concerned.' After this, she sunk into a sullen, defeated silence until she was led away.

As they sat, bemused at the melodrama of what had just

happened, Holmes once again enquired about the dreadful noise that had so distracted Pippa and allowed Garden to disarm her, thus saving both their lives.

'I'd been thinking of our grand opening,' he started. 'I thought we should have something special to mark the occasion, then I decided that maybe it might be good to have something that would attract attention, and then I remembered the impact Geoffrey Jones had made on both of us.'

'Who, in the name of all that is holy, is Geoffrey Jones?' Holmes was well confused now.

'The man who plays the bagpipes. I bumped into him in a corridor on my way to the kitchen earlier, and he said he was due to leave tomorrow. Anyway, I got to thinking how much attention it would attract if we had a piper in full Highland gear outside the shop for the grand opening day, so later on I went to his room and asked him if he'd consider being paid to play outside.

'When he said he would, I arranged for him to have an audition by playing outside your room at exactly five o'clock this afternoon. I knew we'd be talking in private, and I'd decided that, if necessary, I'd *make* it happen there and not outside having a puff.'

'You could've warned me. I nearly had a heart attack when I heard that awful row.'

'I couldn't say anything. This was to see how much it attracted your attention, and how effective you thought it might be in getting people curious about what sort or business the piper was playing outside of.'

'You finished that sentence with a preposition, my boy.'

'I know, and I'm dreadfully sorry: it won't happen again, but you get my meaning.'

'Indeed I do. Tell him he's hired. He'll certainly be a crowd-drawing novelty, and even if no one comes inside to make enquiries, I bet a lot of them might come in for a business card, or will take down the telephone number. We owe our lives to your odd idea and that man's dreadful playing. The least we can do is to say thank you by giving him a whole day in which to play, when no one will complain.'

'When do we open, then?'

'Saturday. The day after tomorrow. It's as good a day as any other, don't yer think?'

Garden gulped. There was really nothing he could think of to say. He was absolutely speechless with the audacity of the man with whom he would now spend his working days.

As if this wasn't enough information to swallow, there was a sharp knock at the door, and Holmes opened it to reveal a positive plethora of representatives of the forces of law and order. Standing in a row as if waiting for a free kick to be aimed at them, were Streeter, Port, and Moriarty, all with grim expressions on their faces.

Streeter pushed his way past Holmes and into the room, his minions following him like bridesmaids. He put his hands behind his back and glared at the two bemused men and drew a long, shuddering breath before launching into his tirade of wrath.

"What the hell did you two think you were doing?" he asked, but the question was evidently rhetorical, for he carried straight on. "You've been meddling in police business and in things that don't concern you at all. Do you hear me? They were none of your business. The likes of the deaths here are for us to sort out, not for amateurs to poke their noses into and put their lives at risk. Do you know how close you came to being dead today?"

Again, this was a rhetorical question, for he merely carried on berating them. "Do you realise the danger you put yourselves in, and other people could easily have become involved by accident and been injured, or even killed. I will not tolerate members of the public poking around in official matters, and I hope you hear me loud and clear, for I never want to find myself in this situation again."

As he paused for breath, Holmes put his hand into his pocket and, in the glare of Garden's horrified gaze, removed one of their business cards and handed it to the inspector in a very sanguine manner.

Streeter read it, and his eyes began to bulge with fury, his face to turn almost purple, his hands to tremble with complete fury. "I won't have it! I simply won't have it, I tell you. I won't tolerate you snooping about in my manor like a pair of Mike Hammers."

'But our premises will be open to the public on Saturday,' Holmes almost purred at him.

'If I catch you investigating anything more serious than a missing cat, dog, or straying spouse, I won't be responsible for my actions. I absolutely forbid you to get mixed up in anything else of a criminal nature, do you hear me?'

'Perfectly, old boy,' replied Holmes. "Now, we'll make statements later but, if you'll excuse us, I think we deserve a large drink after solving this case for you.'

'Solving this case? Why you arrogant, pompous ...' But he never got the chance to finish this sentence, as the other two policeman took an arm each, and almost carried him out of the door and down the corridor, still metaphorically spitting chips.

'Bar, old chap?' enquired Holmes of a very shaken Garden.

'I could certainly do with a drink after all that's happened,' replied his partner, already heading for the door.

Chapter Sixteen

Friday

First thing on Friday morning, they both took their cars to Garden's old address; as they had not found time to do this yet, it was imperative that they get his stuff moved to Holmes' apartment before they opened for business, as the flat would not be ready for occupation for some time. Holmes, trying to take his friend's mind off what lay ahead, stated that he thought he might adopt wearing a deerstalker when they were operational, unless they were undercover, and he really must organise some violin lessons – 'I've got one on the wall at home. I don't know if you noticed it' – just so that he knew the basics, and how to use a bow – that sort of thing.

'And, did I ever tell you what my mother's maiden name was?'

'No,' mumbled a very uncomfortable Garden.

'Go on, have a guess.'

'Can't.'

'It was only Barratt. Imagine if she'd done what a lot of young ladies do nowadays, and hyphenated her maiden name with her married name. I'd be Mr Barratt-Holmes. Unbearable!' Holmes had done his best, but it hadn't been nearly enough to cheer up Garden's gloomy countenance.

Garden gave a weak laugh, but then sunk back into his misery. He hated going back, but had assumed that his mother would be at work on a Friday morning.

She wasn't, and was having a day off from her

temping, and greeted both of them with a radiant smile of welcome. She even helped John H. take his possessions out to the two waiting cars, explaining to nosy neighbours who had come outside to have a look at such an amount of ladies' finery being shifted, that she was clearing out her wardrobes, as she had far too many clothes, and she felt it was time for a change.

For this, Garden was grateful, as he didn't want the neighbours gossiping about him, and they were a really talkative crowd and very judgemental about people. When the cars were fully loaded, Mummy Dearest – aka Shirley – called them both in for large mugs of tea and a full biscuit barrel, as they probably were low on blood sugar after all that running around.

Holmes sat on the sofa and made very acceptable small talk, all the while smiling at Garden's mother, and making rather an old fool of himself, and Garden was glad when they were on their way to Farlington Market and Quaker Street.

At the other end, everything had to happen in reverse, and all the clothes, shoes, make-up, jewellery, and wigs were just dumped in the spare bedroom until there was an opportunity to put everything away. Before that could happen, though, Holmes insisted that he throw them together a ploughman's lunch, and opened a couple of bottles of beer, for he felt they had earned this reward.

Garden was grateful for the offer and sat down at the table as Holmes brought in two plates loaded with hunks of bread, cheese, pickled onions, and chutney, with a dainty garnish of salad. The man had evidently made a quick trip to a local shop while Garden was still in the bedroom working out where everything should go.

He had applied plentiful butter to his bread, and was just about to cut off a small piece of cheese with which to adorn it, when something whizzed across his lap, he felt the sting of needle-sharp claws on his free hand, and when he looked down, his cheese was gone, his hand bleeding, and Colin the cat was sitting on the other side of the room, hunkered down over his ill-gotten gains with a completely different sort of relish.

'Sorry about that, old chap. I'll get you a plaster and some more cheese. I should have mentioned that Colin's a sucker for a bit of mature cheddar. I ought to have given him a piece of it to distract him, but it slipped my mind. Head's in the clouds for some reason.'

Garden sucked his injured hand and glared at the cat. He could see the clouds of war forming on the horizon, and hoped he would not be staying here too long, delightful as the apartment was, because he could never envisage he and Colin becoming the best of friends, or even calling a truce.

When he did get another hunk of cheese, he crouched over it like a dog protecting a precious bone, and didn't sit up straight again until he'd finished eating. He was damned if that animal was going to get another dairy freebie from him, but he did feel better for a full stomach, and was willing to believe that the cat didn't bear him any personal malice, and that it was really the attractions of the cheese that had caused him to scratch his hand in his eagerness to get at the tasty titbit.

As Holmes cleared the table, Garden stood up and stretched, feeling quite achy after all the to-ing and froing, and was suddenly caused to yell out loud, as a series of tiny knives made their way up his legs and spine. When Holmes ran in at the cry of distress, it was to find Colin wrapped around Garden's neck like an old-fashioned fox fur, only much bigger, and much, much heavier, and with much more evil intent.

'See, he likes you, Garden,' Holmes smiled happily at his new lodger.

'No he doesn't,' replied Garden. 'He's gone round in a complete circle and, is at this very ... ow! ... moment, biting my ear. Ouch! Get off, you vicious bugger.'

'Come along, Colin,' Holmes said in a singsong voice. 'John here doesn't know you very well yet, but he knows you love him.'

'Oh no I don't. That cat's got it in for me,' retorted Garden, trying to look over his shoulder for tell-tale blood stains.

'He just doesn't know his own strength.'

'Oh yes he does. And he knows how to use it, too. I bet my back's covered in punctures.'

'He was just showing you that he loved you after you so thoughtfully shared your lunch with him.'

'He was doing nothing of the sort. He was intent on injury from the moment he first saw me, and I don't think he's ever going to become genuinely fond of me.'

'Have you ever had a cat?'

'No, but I know an enemy when I see one.'

Colin, enormous beast that he was, was now on Holmes' lap, padding at his burgeoning paunch blissfully, and purring, but he must have known they were talking about him, because he stopped momentarily and made a wheezy sound, almost like a chuckle, and glared triumphantly at his new adversary.

'I'm going through to put away some of my stuff. If you want me I'll be in the spare room,' Garden declared huffily, realising that Colin would always be Holmes' blind spot. He'd keep a truce so long as the cat played along, but one claw in the wrong place, and he was going to cuff his ears for him good and proper. The animal had no self-discipline, and was obviously spoilt rotten.

When most of his stuff was stored or in suitcases, Holmes breezed into the room heartily and declared he had made an appointment with a decorator to discuss doing up the flat, and then they'd go out to eat. That was fine with Garden. Whenever he'd left the room for a quick visit to the bathroom, he had been aware of being observed hostilely from a number of different places of concealment, and it was making him jumpy. A break from the apartment was just what he needed to restore his courage where that mangy monster was concerned.

The 'decorator' lived in the really posh area on the outskirts of Farlington Market where even the price of an ice-lolly would be sky-high, if there were an ice-cream van classy enough to brave making tinkling calls there. Even the thought of the cost of such luxurious and sprawling accommodation made Garden's eyes water, but Holmes seemed not in the slightest intimidated, but this was probably because he could afford to buy up any one of them without batting an eyelid. Garden didn't have such self-confidence, however, and found himself almost cringing as Holmes pulled a very fancy pull in the porch at the target address.

The man who answered the door was a brawny fellow wearing paint-stained overalls, who looked a bit like an ex-wrestler. His hair was cut to 'number two', if not 'number one' shortness, and he looked very intimidating. Garden was about to ask if the owner was at home when Holmes held out a hand and said, 'Busman's holiday, Mr Legrove?'

This? *This* apparition was Legrove the well-known interior designer of whom even Garden had heard? Why wasn't he dressed in velvet and wearing a cravat? Why was he so brawny and coarse-looking? How could this man be capable of such genius of design? Garden shrugged and followed Holmes into the house, totally at a loss, many of his illusions about interior design shattered. Weren't interior designers supposed to be willowy and foppish, and why hadn't Holmes looked for a simple painter and decorator?

The hall was, indeed, covered in decorating sheets, and open pots of paint stood around like sly traps for the unwary, but when Legrove shrugged off his overalls, the room he showed them into was sublime, and John H. blushed at the *faux pas* he had nearly committed by asking for the householder. People came in all shapes and sizes, and he had been guilty of stereotyping, something he thought he would never do, considering his alter ego.

'Let me show you some colour charts and swatches of material. If you want to pick up some period furniture for the flat, there's an auction next week that I think would be right up your street. I've been given a little peek at some of the stuff and, although it may not come cheap, it's simply divine.'

Garden felt right outside his comfort zone, being more used to flat-pack than drop-dead gorgeous. And to hear the man's deep, rough voice and down-market accent utter the words 'simply divine' sent his head into a whirl of confused thoughts. Holmes, however, was flipping through swatches of curtain and upholstery material, and pawing his way through colour charts, deep in conversation with Legrove, absolutely in his element. Garden would be glad to get back to the apartment, even with his arch-enemy Colin-the-Destroyer in residence. The cat may even be out on the prowl somewhere, torturing and killing some innocent small mammal, if he was lucky.

On the journey back to Quaker Street, Garden was silent and thoughtful for so long that Holmes eventually asked him, 'What did you think of Legrove? He's a bit of a character, isn't he?'

'You can say that again. I nearly asked to see the householder.'

'A lot of people do that, but he's got such a flair for colour and design that he's becoming all the rage. I was lucky to get to see him at such short notice, but he'd had a cancellation and was filling in time working on his own home. It'll be a while before you can move in though. The best has to be, and is worth, waiting for.'

Garden sighed, and decided that it would be as well to purchase some gauntlets.

'Chin up!' Holmes exhorted him. 'We open tomorrow, or had you forgotten?'

Garden had, and sighed again. He felt like he was caught up in a whirlwind. His life had always been quiet, measured, and lived in little compartments before, now he was lurching from one activity to another, and things were moving on apace. He just hoped he could keep up with everything. If not, he wanted to go back to Kansas – he had the ruby slippers back in Holmes' place.

Once again in the apartment, Holmes headed straight for the shower, and Garden went to his room to sort out something more suitable to dinner out than the casual clothes he had worn for the work they had done today. There had been no sign of the cat, but on entering his room, Garden's nose began to twitch, and it wasn't long before his eyes told him too that Colin had paid the lodger's new domain a visit. Right there in one of his blood-red Italian leather shoes was a deposit, but not the sort that would be appreciated by a bank. The cat had taken a dump in his shoes, and that was the second time that his beautiful shoes had had something disgusting thrust all over – or in this case, in – them, in just a few days. They'd definitely have to be burnt now. Maybe he could use the gas poker.

'Holmes!' he squeaked in disgust and despair. Those shoes had cost him a week's wages. 'I demand that you clean up after your perfectly horrid animal.'

Holmes hurried out of the shower as quickly as he could, and took away the despoiled articles, promising to return them as good as new, but Garden couldn't somehow see himself ever having the stomach to wear them again without the thought of what had been in them and on them.

He took Holmes' place in the bathroom, feeling glad the offending animal hadn't been around. If it had he would probably have kicked it into the middle of next week. He'd have to pin his hopes on Legrove getting another cancellation, for if he had to live with this sort of disdainful treatment from a mere cat, he could see felicide being committed, and his partnership with the owner would not last very long after that, what with Garden having killed Daddy's little darling.

When he had finished his ablutions, he came out to find the apartment abandoned by both its furry and its non-furry resident, so he made himself a cup of tea and sat down to read an abandoned copy of a newspaper that Holmes had picked up when they went out earlier. He had had quite an upheaval in the last twenty-four hours, and he needed a period of respite in which to start the recovery process before he got involved in what would be the whirl of opening the office doors for the first time the next morning.

It was six o'clock before Holmes returned to change, and at six-thirty he deposited his car keys on the hallstand and announced that a taxi would be picking them up very shortly, and that they would be eating in a pub called The Sherlock, which he had discovered by accident one day when searching for an address he never found. The pub itself was a gem, done up in the true Edwardian manner, and with lots of Holmes aficionados as regulars.

Garden was astounded when they reached their destination, there were deer-stalkers a-plenty, violins and bows on the walls, and many a rack of pipes, both meerschaum and Basil Rathbone-style, strewn about the place's stage-dressing. And it was only about a mile from Quaker Street but, as Holmes explained, they would want wine with their meal and it would be an inauspicious start to a career in private investigation if it began with being caught for driving over the limit, and he couldn't have been more right.

The hours passed only too quickly and, all too soon they found themselves back at the door of the apartment. 'I think I'll take myself straight up the wooden hill to Bedfordshire,' announced Holmes, who didn't actually possess a staircase, and headed for his bedroom door. Garden was totally in agreement, and, turning towards the door of his own room, went inside.

Colin had evidently been in during the evening, and he must remember to keep the door to his room shut, for this time the little bugger had peed all down the pair of slacks he had left out for the grand opening in the morning. Once again the cat had got one over on him. His hands, completely independently of his brain, made strangling motions in the air. He'd get his own back, one of these days, you just see if he didn't.

From his own room, his partner was just taking off his shirt when he heard the anguished cry from the other bedroom. 'Holmes! He's done it again.'

Chapter Seventeen

Saturday

They were both early into the new offices the next morning, and once more they surveyed, with pride, the job they had done furnishing it. The front office looked modern and professional; the back office, in total contrast, had that 'old, steady, trustworthy, established firm' look. The desks were on the left and right walls as one entered, and against the opposite wall, with only a break for the door which formed the back entrance, were oak filing cabinets, stacked to give the appearance of a giant pharmacist's cabinet.

One of the large rugs they had also bought at the auction looked stunning across the middle of the floor, and Holmes had also found two wing chairs in leather for the client's to sit in while they consulted with their chosen detective. In a corner stood a large coat and hat stand with, Garden noticed, a deerstalker – as threatened – hanging from it, as well as a cloaked overcoat and, hung on the wall, was what, the younger man presumed, was a second violin. It was all so reminiscent of the pub they had visited the previous evening that Garden realised that Holmes *was* taking the whole thing seriously, in his own, unique way, but that he had lapses of concentration, and was liable to fly off, for a while, on a tangent.

Glancing his eyes around the rest of the back office, he noticed that there were gilt-framed pictures on the wall, and a venerable old clock ticked on the wall. It felt like a long-lost home, and definitely had the atmosphere that would make it easy for a person with a problem with which they could assist to unburden themselves. It certainly inspired trust and confidence.

The piper also turned up early, and went up to the empty flat upstairs to get his instrument tuned up and ready to play. He was resplendent, as promised, in full Highland regalia, looking absolutely fantastic, and would certainly cause a stir playing out in the main street. It was an auspicious start. If only the rest of the day could go as well.

At nine o'clock sharp, their piper took himself off to being playing, and he could be heard greeting somebody as he went through the door. Both men stood still, a small smile playing about Holmes' lips.

'Is that a client already?' asked Garden, his stomach turning over nervously.

'I think I know who it is,' replied Holmes, who was now definitely smirking. 'If I'm not mistaken, I should be able to introduce you to our new receptionist/secretary.'

Garden's stomach gave another involuntary flip, and he unconsciously checked his appearance in the gilt-framed mirror which was hung next to the door to the outer office for just that purpose. When on earth had the man had time to sort this out?

Holmes held the door open to usher his partner through, saying at the same time, 'May I introduce you to our newest member of staff, Ms Shirley Garden.'

Holmes had only gone and hired his mother, who was supposed to be happily temping her way to a living without any complaint. 'When the hell did this happen?' demanded Garden in a croaky voice tinged with shock.

'When I nipped out, when you were in the shower yesterday evening. Your mother is always very well presented, and I thought she would be the ideal front image for our new venture. She's neither an air-headed youngster, nor a gorgon-headed old monster. What do you think?'

Garden thought nothing. For the first time in his life, he had passed out cold. He couldn't wait to get away from living with his mother, and now he was going to spend every day working in the same offices as her. He must have been very evil in a past life – maybe Vlad the Impaler – for this was his worst nightmare come true.

When he returned to consciousness, he found himself in the secretary's chair where Holmes had managed to haul his unresisting body, his mother was fanning his face with a clean tea towel, and in the spare seat intended for clients who came in to enquire about their services, was a woman weeping copiously, and bleating that they just had to help her, because she couldn't stand it any more.

It looked like their very first official case had walked through the door and, as it were, caught them with their pants down. Outside, the piper was playing a lament, having switched from the lively tones of a reel, and it set the tone horribly accurately.

They had to look professional and experienced, they had to do it confidently, and, more than that, they had to do it *now*!

THE END

Other titles
by
Andrea Frazer

  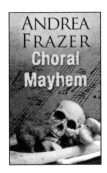

For more information about **Andrea Frazer**
and other **Accent Press** titles
please visit
www.accentpress.co.uk